ANYTHING GHOST

A REAPER WITCH MYSTERY: BOOK 8

ELLE ADAMS

To be notified when Elle Adams's next book is released, sign up to her author newsletter.

"This is a bad idea," my ghostly brother, Mart, whispered in my ear.

"I'm aware."

I pushed my foot down into the river, trying to suppress a shudder of discomfort as the cold water flowed over the top of my boot. Then I did the same with the other foot and took careful steps forward until I stood amid the gushing current. October wasn't the best time to wade into a river that was deadly on a good day, but this was the first time since summer that the water levels were low enough to risk going in search of the tunnel again.

Biting my tongue to avoid focusing on the ongoing chill of the water soaking into my socks, I followed the bank of the river towards the bridge that connected one side of Hawkwood Hollow to the other. As I craned my neck to see into the shadows under the bridge where I knew the tunnel was located, Mart came floating past, his transparent feet skimming the water.

"It's still covered," he announced.

"Partly." I could see the hole in the ground that led to the tunnel above the lapping waters, and while the notion of crawling into the tunnel after nearly drowning a few weeks ago was unappealing, I'd been waiting for this moment for what felt like forever.

"Maura," said a voice from the bridge, "what are you doing?"

Jia. I'd hoped my co-worker wouldn't notice my little excursion, but there she was, peering down from above, her straight dark hair blowing sideways in the breeze.

"Just having a look around," I called up to her. "The water level is down. I can see the underside of the bridge again."

"You aren't going in there, are you?" She ran to the other side of the bridge and began to make her way down the slope of the riverbank to join me. "Maura?"

"I'm not," I said ineffectually. "I'm looking."

"Of course you are." She reached the edge of the bank and placed her hands on her hips. "Maura, do you not remember the last time?"

"With all too much clarity." Thanks to a spell someone had carved into the tunnel walls, my Reaper powers had been cut off, preventing me from getting out. I'd almost died. "Nobody's been in there since the last time. They won't have had time to put up any more anti-Reaper defences."

Reapers were normally indestructible by nature. Collecting the souls of the dead and delivering them to the afterlife wasn't a job any old human could do, and to do that job, we needed to be able to get into places where normal people couldn't survive. Someone, however, had tried to find a way around those rules—someone closely tied to the reason I'd needed to get into the tunnel in the first place.

"Still." Jia peered over the bank's edge, her mouth tight with concern. "It's dangerous. There's no telling what other defences were put in there by whoever created the tunnel to stop anyone going snooping."

No kidding. The tunnel was just one part of my plan to investigate the misdeeds of Mina Devlin, former leader of Hawkwood Hollow's sole witch coven, who'd been responsible for countless crimes over her decades of leadership. Unfortunately, she'd been equally adept at hiding said crimes by covering up all the evidence. None of us had guessed that a massive clue lay right beneath our feet, covered by earth and floodwater. No one knew about the tunnel but her followers, one of whom had been responsible for trying to drown me, and I had every intention of finding out which one.

"I can go snooping instead," Mart announced. "I'm not afraid of a bit of water."

"You're volunteering?" I asked in surprise. Mart was usually a pain to negotiate with. He wanted payment in exchange for doing me any favours, which generally took the form of hot showers because my brother was the weirdest ghost in existence.

"Obviously not for free," he said, "but I'm not pulling your drowned body out of the river again."

Oh. Right. When I'd nearly drowned, it would have spelled the end for my brother as well. In complete defiance of the Reapers' rules and the reason I'd left their ranks, Mart's ghost was tethered to me, which meant when I died, he'd be pulled into the permanent afterlife along with me. "What do you want in exchange? I'm pretty sure you have the monopoly on our choices of movie-night entertainment for the next decade already."

"And there are only so many showers you can take before Allie's hot water bills go through the roof," said Jia.

"Don't give him ideas." I gave Mart an expectant look. "Well?"

"If I do this for you," he said, "you have to give me a leading role in the Halloween event."

"That's up to Carey, not me, but fine." In truth, I'd already planned to give him centre stage in our biggest event of the year. He might be insufferable sometimes, but he liked nothing more than attention, and the big Halloween extravaganza would provide a sizeable audience for his antics.

"Good." Mart flew into the darkness under the bridge and vanished through the half-submerged tunnel opening.

Jia and I watched him for a moment before she turned and eyed me. "Your face is turning blue, Maura."

"It's bloody freezing in here." I didn't want to let the tunnel opening out of my sight, nor did I like thinking of my brother being alone, surrounded by those narrow walls and slimy floors, covered in the old bones of the long dead and the etched glyphs of deadly magic.

Several minutes later, Mart emerged, shaking himself off as if he were soaking wet and not me. "Well, that was boring."

"What do you mean?" I climbed out of the river, shivering, and took Jia's proffered hand to climb up the muddy bank.

"There's nothing in there that I could see." He easily glided up to join us. "Aside from the markings on the walls, but if they're designed to react to trespassers, ghosts don't count."

"Any… bodies?" I faltered.

"Bones, yes. Old ones."

Figures. The bodies wouldn't be identifiable, since they were most likely victims of the flood that occurred more than two decades ago. Because one of the victims had been the local Reaper's apprentice, the Reaper had resigned from his job, which was the reason the town was full of more ghosts than the average place. Then I'd shown up and caused him to reluctantly admit that the real culprit of the floods was none other than Mina Devlin.

Not that I'd *told* anyone that. There never seemed to be a

good time to bring up the subject, and as I hadn't lived here twenty years ago when the river had burst its banks, explaining how I knew would result in putting a spotlight on the notoriously surly local Reaper. Also, certain police officers looked askance at anything other than hard evidence. Ghost testimony didn't count, supposedly, and none of them could recall the events of the flood regardless. Mina had seen to that.

"Creepy," said Jia. "Did you see any hints at which sneaky person tried to drown Maura?"

"Nope," Mart replied. "If you ask me, we should set up an ambush in case they decide to come back to resume their shenanigans."

Hmm. Who was it? It didn't necessarily matter; Mina had a large number of allies, some of whom had left Hawkwood Hollow and some of whom might still be here, for all I knew. The trouble was that nobody would outright *admit* to being one of her supporters.

The sound of approaching footsteps came from the bridge, followed by a snide voice. "What are you two doing down there?"

Suppressing a groan, I lifted my head. On the bridge stood my least favourite police officer, Petra. Her blond hair fell in curtains on either side of her stern face as she regarded us with the look of a headmistress who'd cornered a couple of misbehaving pupils smoking behind the bike shed.

"Nothing whatsoever," Jia answered, which was technically true. "What're *you* doing here?"

"That's no way to talk to an officer of the law," Petra said haughtily. "It looks to me like you're trespassing."

"Trespassing?" I echoed. "Does someone own the riverbank now?"

"I'd have thought you'd be more careful, Reaper," she said. "That tunnel is dangerous, and it's also off-limits to the public. I thought I made that clear to you after the incident a few weeks ago."

Had she? She might have said something to that effect, but I'd been too out of it to pay her much attention.

"The tunnel's still flooded," I told her. "You can look for yourself. We haven't set foot in there, so there's not going to be anything for you to find."

"If that's the case, why are you here?"

Mart blew a raspberry at her. It was probably for the best that she had no ability to see or hear ghosts, though if she did, she might have taken me a bit more seriously.

"I do live here, remember?" I pointed behind me at the Riverside Inn, farther up the slope. "I saw the water levels were lower and wanted to make sure nobody was making trouble in there."

"That is up to the police, not you," Petra said. "You're a known troublemaker yourself, Reaper. Now, leave."

"That wasn't nice," said Mart. "Maybe we should push her into the river."

Please don't. From his grin, he'd figured out what I was thinking, though we weren't speaking mind to mind as we'd done weeks ago in the tunnel. That had been a link forged out of desperation. I still wasn't sure how to replicate it—or if I wanted to. I didn't need to hear my brother's thoughts any more than he needed to hear mine.

"Fine," I said to Petra. "Let me know if you need me to banish anything nasty you might find in there."

I left before she could reply, reasonably sure that she'd sooner let a zombie strangle her to death than ask for my help. I was pretty sure she'd gone as far as to call the Wardens a few weeks ago to get me kicked out of town, and while the Wardens and I had ended up working together, that didn't change the fact that someone among the local law enforcement didn't want a Reaper butting into police business. Never mind that I'd *helped* the police on more than one occasion. I was also dating the head of the local police force, Drew, who wasn't too happy that one of his officers was willing to go to any lengths to discredit me. But if he pushed too far, his own position would be in jeopardy.

"I bet the other officers won't stand for it," Jia remarked to me as we turned our backs on the river. "Would they like hanging around outside in the cold to guard a tunnel nobody can get into?"

"You'd think not." I used my wand to dry myself before walking the rest of the way to the Riverside Inn, where Jia and I worked. The inn was also my home, which was another reason I hoped the police wouldn't take up residence outside its doors. "I'll call Drew and make sure he knows."

An array of Halloween decorations greeted us inside the restaurant that stood adjacent to the inn itself, connected to the lobby by a set of automatic doors. Carey had been adding new decorations every day since October had begun, with the result that there was hardly an inch of wall that wasn't plastered in faux horror-movie posters while most of the corners were full of fake spiderwebs and other paraphernalia. Mart's favourite was the inflatable pumpkin, which he liked to wear on his head while parading in front of our guests on our twice-weekly ghost tours.

Our major event would be on the final day of October itself, and given the rate at which Carey's enthusiasm kept increasing, I was a little concerned that I'd wake up one morning to find that she'd hired a plethora of actors to dress as zombies for the night or something. She was already trying to convince Jia and me to dress up for the occasion, though I drew the line at wearing a black cloak and carrying a rubber scythe.

At least she was having fun. I wasn't the biggest fan of Halloween myself—or Samhain, as the witches called it—as it was the one night of the year when the barriers between the earth and the afterworld were thin enough that ghosts who weren't usually able to show their faces could cross over. As if I didn't see enough ghosts already. Until this year, my plans for Samhain had generally involved taking a sleeping pill and passing out while Mart partied with the other ghosts who came back for the night, but I doubted Carey would let me get away with skipping out on the inn's biggest event of the year.

Allie smiled when she saw Jia and me walk into the restaurant. She'd added pumpkin-shaped clips to her glasses, and the hat perched atop her grey-streaked dark hair was adorned with spiderwebs. "There you two are. Ready for the tour tonight?"

"Sure." At this point, our regular tour routine was old hat. It was Halloween that we needed to be prepared for. "Is Carey?"

"Yes, though I have to keep reminding her it isn't Halloween yet," said Allie. "She needs to save some of her energy for then."

"Pretty sure she has plenty going spare." I envied Carey's ebullience sometimes, not to mention her teenage ability to forego sleep to work on last-minute preparations and not look like a walking zombie, as I generally did.

The inn's resident ghosts were equally excited for the big night. As Jia and I prepared for our shift, we watched Jonathan, our resident expert in conjuring up creepy shadows, practising an imitation of a spider crawling up the wall. Brian, whose ability to freeze water saved our need for an ice-cube dispenser, also watched Jonathan. I assumed Wade and Louise were in the games room watching TV. The older couple, who teamed up to create spooky effects for our guests using doors and lighting, had sort of adopted the youngest ghost, Vicky, which was adorable. Vicky herself was our guests' current favourite ghost, much to Mart's eternal annoyance, and I suspected his plan to take a starring role on Halloween events was part of his ongoing attempt to claim the top spot for himself.

Soon enough, Jia and I were busy serving customers who wanted a taste of our seasonal menu. Carey had updated every drink and snack for the month with a new twist, and I was adding pumpkin-shaped sprinkles to yet another latte when Jia made a sudden noise of surprise and dropped the spoon she was holding. "What's *she* doing here?"

"Who?" I raised my head to see Jennifer Ness, the current Hawkwood Hollow coven leader, crossing the room with a determined air. *Weird.* I handed off the latte to the customer and waited for her to approach. Jennifer had never come to the inn before. I'd gotten the impression that the restaurant wasn't really her scene, and the witches in general had avoided the place ever since I'd ousted Mina Devlin from her position. The well-dressed coven leader with her elaborately styled hair looked decidedly out of place amid the garish posters and pumpkins.

"This is a bit much, isn't it?" she remarked.

"Hey, don't knock Carey's decorations," Jia said, her tone carefully neutral. "She's fifteen. Anyway, what d'you want, a latte?"

"No, I'd like to talk to Maura."

"Really?" It was my turn to tense. "How exactly can I help you?"

She looked me in the eyes. "I have a task that I think only you can help me with. It's urgent."

Oh boy.

2

"What do you mean?" The coven leader needed *my* help? "Do you want me to summon a ghost?"

"No." Jennifer briefly scanned the room and lowered her voice. "Something has been stolen from the coven's head-quarters. A book."

My brows shot up. "A *book?*"

"A dangerous one," she added. "Stolen from Mina Devlin's old office, to be precise."

Okay, maybe that was worth kicking up a fuss over. "Who do you think stole it? One of her allies?"

"I have my suspicions."

Why does she need me, though? "Is there a reason you came to me and not the police? I don't know the identity of every person in the coven, let alone who supported Mina and who didn't."

"Nevertheless," she said, "I need your help, and I'd be happy to compensate you accordingly."

"I'm not a detective. You want Drew for that." Why hadn't she just called the police instead? I'd been reprimanded by the *actual* police only a few hours prior, which was reason enough for me to stay out of this. If she needed a Reaper specifically… All right, maybe I was more likely to say yes than old Harold, but that didn't necessarily make me the right person for the job.

Annoyance flickered across her face. "This isn't something the police can help with. I need a witch, one without ties."

"To the coven?" Jia guessed. "Why, exactly?"

"For the interest of neutrality," she replied.

Translation: she didn't trust the other coven members. *That* was a revelation.

"I'm only half-witch," I pointed out. "Also, most of your coven members hate me for driving off your former leader."

"I'll do most of the questioning myself."

Hmm. "I'll consider it, but I doubt anyone is going to confess to stealing from you in front of me."

"I can offer you compensation." She smiled tightly. "If you do this for me, I'll hold my post-coven meetings at the Riverside Inn instead of the Crooked Broomstick."

My mouth dropped open. "What?"

Admittedly, I was surprised she'd kept using the Crooked Broomstick for coven gatherings even after her predecessor had left town, as the dingy pub was in dire need of refurbishment, but the other witches would probably rather meet in the cemetery than gather here at the inn.

"I'm sure your boss will be glad of the business," Jennifer went on. "You can let me know your answer later."

She walked out of the restaurant, while Jia and I gawked after her. Even the ghosts stared, including Mart, who'd completely forgotten the pumpkin-shaped balloon he'd been levitating. I hastened to retrieve the balloon before it knocked over someone's drink and then returned to the counter.

"What in the hell was that?" asked Jia.

"I wish I knew." I tied the balloon's string to the tap to prevent it from drifting off. "Do you think she actually wants my help?"

"You know, I think she does," she said. "She wouldn't have come here if she didn't."

Weirder and weirder. "I don't get it. She doesn't require a Reaper to catch a thief."

Jia shrugged. "She could have asked that ridiculous assistant of hers, but I guess you're more competent than she is."

True enough. Wendy was a complete wet flannel of a witch who was about as equipped to take on Mina Devlin as Petra was to befriend a ghost.

Speaking of whom… "I wonder if she saw the police on the way?"

"No idea." She shook her head. "We should tell Allie. I don't think she'd object if the witches bring more business here, but I don't know that she wants the entire coven swarming the place either."

"No, she definitely doesn't," I said. "They can keep those karaoke nights of theirs to the Crooked Broomstick instead. Can you imagine them trying to cross the river while inebriated?"

Jia snorted. "Yeah, that's bound to end badly."

Nevertheless, Jennifer must be desperate to catch the culprit if she'd been willing to enlist *my* help. That or she must suspect someone close to her of being the thief.

"Who was that?" Allie walked into the restaurant, sparing us from having to seek her out. "Was that the head of the coven?"

"Yes, it was," I said. "Jennifer wanted to 'hire' me to find a missing book. If I do it, she'll raise our image in the eyes of the coven."

"Will she?" Her brow furrowed. "That seems… odd. What book?"

"She wouldn't say." I glanced at Jia. "She's given me time to make up my mind, but I don't know that I want to commit to anything without knowing more."

"What if someone close to her stole the book?" Jia put in, echoing my earlier thought. "What if Wendy did it?"

"I don't picture her as a thief, do you?" I asked. The nervous, hand-wringing witch who followed Jennifer everywhere like a shadow was possibly the unlikeliest candidate. "Nah, it's got to be one of Mina's former cronies. Whoever is left."

I needed to message Drew and see what *he* thought of it all. I'd texted him at the start of the workday to tell him about the police showing up at the river, but that was before Jennifer Ness's unexpected visit.

"Strange," Allie said. "Well, I wouldn't object to making peace with the coven, and Carey certainly wouldn't mind the extra business."

"I guess." I didn't particularly want more attention on the inn, but I knew Jennifer was trying to build a new coven on her own terms—which was a tad difficult with the shadow of Mina Devlin eternally hanging over the town. We were better off without her, if you asked me, but nobody ever did ask me.

By the time Drew showed up an hour or so into my shift, Jia, Mart, and I had exhausted all possible arguments for and against helping the coven, so I was glad to have someone to add impartial input. Granted, it might be a stretch to call Drew "impartial."

Tall and broad, Drew had the typical shifter appearance, except with longish dark hair instead of blond, and he looked somewhat out of place amid all the Halloween décor. "I swear there are twice as many fake spiders as the last time I came in," he remarked as he reached the bar. "I didn't see any officers, though. Who…?"

"Petra," I said. "She took issue with Jia and me going near the river. She said the tunnel is out-of-bounds now that the water levels are low enough that we might be able to get in."

"You *didn't* go into the tunnel, did you?"

"No." When he sighed, I added, "I waded in a little, but I couldn't get into the tunnel itself. I sent Mart instead."

"Maura."

"He's a ghost," I pointed out. "It's perfectly safe."

"You nearly died there."

"I'm aware. So is Petra, but I doubt she's banned me from the area out of concern for my safety."

His gaze clouded. "No, but it is dangerous. We can't have the local kids playing down there."

"They have more sense." I drew in a breath. "You didn't actually ban the public from going into the river, did you? Is this some new rule Petra made up?"

"I didn't," he said, "but she's right. If the tunnel's open again, we need to establish some rules to stop the public from putting themselves in danger."

"I take it you don't object to me sending Mart in, at the very least?" I asked. "As a ghost, he won't trip any magical alarms."

"No, he won't," he said grudgingly. "But that won't be enough for you, will it? I know you, Maura."

He had me there. "I wouldn't take the risk if I didn't think it would be worth it."

"Why?" he asked.

"You know why." I leaned over the counter and lowered my voice. "Something very illegal happened down there that's likely connected to a certain ex-coven leader. I'd like to know what, wouldn't you?"

"Not at the expense of your life," he said. "Besides, we

already have evidence enough against her."

Yeah, but not for her biggest crime. I hadn't spelled it out for him—namely, that the coven had been responsible for causing the floods two decades ago that had caused the town to turn into a haven for ghosts—but I had good reason for withholding the full story. The only person who knew all the details was Harold the Reaper, who'd ordered me not to tell another soul.

The problem was, the coven had had complete control over the local newspapers at the time, and there'd been a well-orchestrated cover-up to the extent that nobody had ever guessed the truth. Harold had never revealed exactly *what* Mina had been trying to do, and he hadn't clued me in about the tunnels until I'd stumbled upon them myself.

"Anyway, I have more news," I said to Drew. "The coven leader decided to hire me to help find a missing book. Have you heard about a robbery at the coven headquarters?"

"No," he said. "Should I have?"

"I guess she didn't want to call the police," I surmised. "I think she's suspicious of her own coven members, but someone took some important book from Mina's old office."

"Mina's office?" he echoed. "She ought to have told the police."

"I'm telling you now, aren't I?"

"Still." His brow pinched. "What book is this?"

"I don't know yet," I said. "She seemed reluctant to tell me the details, but she also said that if I help her, she can mend the inn's reputation in the eyes of the coven. That's no small thing."

"Not if she's asking for something you can't help with," he said. "Why you?"

"I wondered the same thing," I said. "I figured I might as well stop by the coven headquarters and ask a few questions later. It's not as risky as going into a certain tunnel, is it?"

"No, but that doesn't mean it's up to you to solve her problems," he said. "Are you really thinking of saying yes?"

"I don't know. Problems I ignore tend to come back and hit me in the face."

"That's true," Jia put in. "The kind of books Mina's people were interested in aren't the sort you want in the wrong hands."

"Exactly," I said to Drew. "Remember the incident with the book from the old library? The monsters?"

"All too clearly." His expression darkened. "You'll let me know if you do decide to go and talk to them, won't you?"

"Of course," I said. "I won't be able to leave until Carey's back from school anyway."

He inclined his head. "All right. I have to head back to the office. I'll certainly talk to Petra about those tunnels."

"Tell her that if she's so concerned about keeping the public out, she's welcome to lead a team in to explore." The place was booby-trapped to hell—or at least, it had been— but I knew that whatever lay down there was worth the risk. For me, at least.

Drew left, and the rest of the workday passed without any more surprise visitors. By the time Carey came back from school, the crowd had died down enough that I'd decided that I could do worse than to see if Jennifer was willing to reveal more details while we were in the safety of her own office.

Carey bounded into the restaurant and left her bag by a table next to the bar, her mustard-yellow uniform clashing with the Halloween decorations. Casper, her familiar, flopped onto a nearby seat. The cat was a lot calmer around the local ghosts than he used to be, though he still freaked out whenever one of them got too close to him. Carey had been working on helping him with his anxiety issues after he'd spent one of the ghost-tour nights running through the corridors and yowling. Luckily, the guests had thought it was part of the show, but I did feel sorry for the poor cat.

"Hey." I ducked out from behind the bar. "I'm heading out for a bit, but I'll be back long before the tour starts. That okay?"

"Sure." Carey smiled up at me. "Where're you going?"

"To see the coven."

"To see... Wait, did you say the *coven?*"

"Yeah, Jennifer wants a favour," I replied. "I won't be long."

I left through the automatic doors, shivering a little in the cool air. I didn't see Petra or the other police officers anywhere near the tunnel this time, though Mart made a show of peering over the bridge. "She's not there. So much for all her threats."

"Is the tunnel entrance any clearer?" I asked, curious despite myself. "Want to have another look?"

"No and no," he said. "I already had a thorough search, except near the tunnel's other entrance—but don't get any ideas."

"I'm not." Though I'd briefly forgotten that the other entrance to the tunnel was farther up the river, and that it might have been how Mina's ally had slipped into the town to begin with.

Drew might have good reason to be concerned about the danger, but this was personal. Someone had tried to kill me, and I didn't appreciate it one bit.

I entered the magenta-painted building that housed the coven's main base and climbed the staircase to Jennifer's office. To no surprise, Wendy waylaid me, wringing her hands. "Reaper. What are you doing here?"

"Jennifer asked to see me." I moved to the office door and knocked, ignoring Wendy's presence hovering over my shoulder like a particularly persistent ghost. I didn't know if her boss had actually told her about the theft, so I decided against mentioning it unless the coven leader did.

"Come in," Jennifer called.

I opened the door and entered the small room, already having second thoughts about my decision. The office itself was unremarkable, containing bookshelves and cabinets and a wooden desk in the centre, behind which sat the blond coven leader.

"Maura." She gave me a tight nod. "I'm glad you decided to come and help me out."

"I came to hear more details," I corrected. "If I'm to catch the thief, I need to know where to start. Do you have any suspects?"

"I have a few ideas," she replied. "The thief stole from Mina's office, and they did so in a way that was intended to catch my attention. Few people have access to that room."

"Including your own assistant?"

She inclined her head. Wow, she really did suspect Wendy. Though I had to wonder… How many people here were still in contact with Mina Devlin? Was Jennifer's leadership as secure as she believed?

"So you see why I need an impartial outsider involved."

"I appreciate your faith in me," I said, "but *I* don't have that much faith in the rest of the coven to answer my questions. Also, I don't exactly have a surplus of free time. It's two weeks until Halloween."

"Yes, I suppose it is." She glanced down at a stack of papers on her desk. "I spoke to the police earlier, but they said that the break-in must have happened from inside the building."

"You did call the police?" I'd have to check with Drew, but there was no reason for her to lie to me. "They didn't want to get involved?"

"No, but they're limited in their ability to interfere in

what is almost certainly coven business." She drummed her fingers atop the stack of papers. "That said, they *do* seem conflicted over this tunnel... and did I hear that the river's levels are almost low enough for them to search inside?"

My shoulders tensed. "What does the tunnel have to do with the theft?"

She arched a brow. "I thought that's what you wanted— the police to take your claims about the tunnel seriously."

Actually, I wanted them to leave it alone and let me explore it myself. "You'd think my near-drowning would have tipped them off that something was wrong down there. Did *you* know your predecessor had a secret lair right underneath our feet?"

"No," she said. "I did not, but I'm interested in learning more. If you are, too, we can amend our agreement to include that too."

I blinked. "To include what? I'm not going back in there until I'm certain nobody else will try to drown me."

"I'd be willing to assist you," she said, "and if necessary, to persuade the police to undergo a full investigation."

That... would really help. Though it surely couldn't be that easy. "Didn't they just refuse to help you find the thief?"

"I decided not to push the matter," she said. "Like I said, this is a coven issue. However, my predecessor..." She paused. "I'm right in thinking the police have had trouble gathering evidence of her misdeeds?"

I shrugged. Had she been talking to Drew? I'd have to check with him later, but if she was offering to help us find proof, I'd be a fool to pass it up.

"I'm not asking for much," she added. "If any of the people I question today turns out to be the thief and confesses to the crime, I'll maintain my end of the bargain. You won't have to do anything more."

Ah, hell. "Fine."

3

"So," I said in the silence that followed my agreement. "Which individuals do you want to start with?"

"I imagine you might have guessed one person I have some questions for," said Jennifer. "My assistant."

"Wendy?" She actually thought Wendy could be the thief? "Why would she steal from you?"

"Oh, I have my doubts that she's the thief, but she's the last person who was in that room before the book went missing. I put her in charge of keeping an eye on Mina's assets, so if anyone's likely to have seen whoever took the book, it's her."

Well, well. "All right. Should I go and find her?"

"She'll already be outside the room."

Right. She probably was—and had likely been listening to our entire conversation. "Okay, then."

"Wendy?" she called. "Come in."

The door nudged inward, and Wendy came shuffling into the room, wringing her hands so intensely that she looked like she was trying to keep hold of a slippery python. Her

eyes brimmed with dread when she saw me standing opposite her coven leader.

"Yes?" she squeaked.

"I've asked Maura here to help find the missing book that
was taken from our coven headquarters yesterday," said
Jennifer. "Since you're the last person who went into that
room, I think you should give an account of the incident so
that she knows where to start looking. Don't you agree?"

Wendy's round eyes fixated on me. "Why? Why her?"

"I'm asking the questions, Wendy." Jennifer's tone was
almost gentle, but Wendy quailed all the same.

"I didn't mean to question your judgement." Wendy's
voice came out as a squeak again. "I was just—ah—I didn't
see who took the book from Mina's office. I didn't see
anyone."

"Then tell me what you did see. When did you realise the
book was missing?"

"I didn't." She swallowed. "I go in there every day to clean
and dust the shelves, but I don't usually examine them
closely. I didn't realise anything was gone until you came to
me and told me."

I swivelled back to the coven leader. "You went in there
after Wendy did and realised the book was missing? How
many other people have access to that room?"

"Only those who can unlock the door," Jennifer replied.
"The two of us alone hold the key. I usually keep it in my
office."

Weird. I turned back to Wendy, who continued to wring
her hands. Did her nervousness indicate guilt, or was she just
terrified at the concept of getting into trouble with her coven
leader? I was inclined to believe the latter, if just because her
zealous dedication to Jennifer made it unlikely that she'd
commit theft right in front of her leader's nose. Besides,

there was no good reason for Wendy to steal anything from the former coven leader's office, was there?

"Nobody had taken the key before I went in there," Wendy whispered. "It was in its usual place in your desk drawer."

"As you said before." Jennifer pursed her lips. "This leaves me in a difficult position, Wendy. Someone undoubtedly stole from Mina's office, and if they didn't use the key, they must have used magic to get in. There were no signs of interference inside the room?"

Wendy shook her head. "No… no."

"Do you think it was one of her allies?" I asked. "Mina's?"

Wendy flinched, but Jennifer gave a nod. "Whoever it was, they got through a locked door in our headquarters, and they did so without triggering any of the security spells set up around the office to prevent intruders from gaining access."

Wendy coughed. "Can't Reapers walk through walls?"

Thanks for that. "I had zero reason to go into that office. The time I got locked in there was enough to put me off, and I don't even know which book got stolen or why you're so desperate to get it back."

"It's a book of dark magic," Wendy whispered. "Dark magic… the sort that is of interest to Reapers."

"Wendy, Maura has no reason whatsoever to have gone into that office," Jennifer interjected. "Nor could she have known there was a hidden compartment in there."

"Hidden?" I decided to let Wendy's accusation slide, if just because Jennifer clearly didn't believe I was responsible. "You might have mentioned that earlier."

"Mina concealed a compartment in the back of a cabinet," Jennifer clarified. "I didn't know it was there until recently, when Wendy moved the cabinet to vacuum along the back wall of the office."

"You looked inside the compartment before the book was stolen?" I asked. "You already knew about it?"

"I did," Jennifer replied. "I decided a locked office that only two of us had full access to was as safe a hiding place as possible, so I left the book and pushed the cabinet back into place."

"Someone else must have known." I looked between them. "Was anyone else here in the building at the time of the theft?"

"No, not that I know of," said Wendy. "The theft must have taken place overnight, when nobody was at work, but… but anyone can access the coven headquarters at any time."

"Any coven member." Oh, they claimed all witches had access, but when I'd tried to get into the supply cabinets myself, I'd usually been interrogated or thrown out. Honestly, I had a hard time feeling sorry for the witches after the way they'd treated me before Jennifer's ascension to leader. I was also beginning to regret agreeing to help them. "Were either of you here?"

"No," said Wendy. "I—I got here at six o'clock or so. I always arrive shortly before the coven leader, so I can clean and tidy her office."

"Do you have security measures on the building when nobody's here?" I asked.

"We lock the building, yes," said Wendy, "but we don't put any magical defences on the doors. Anyone might want to come in for legitimate reasons, and we have a duty towards our coven members."

Hmm. "Did you see anything else out of place?"

"No…" She cleared her throat. "Ah, but I didn't check any of the other offices. They don't like people going in there without permission, so I only clean the rooms of the coven leader… and her predecessor."

I faced Jennifer. "Do I have this right? Wendy cleaned

Mina's office without realising there'd been a break-in, and then you went in after her and discovered the theft. What made you want to check?"

"Habit," Jennifer said. "Since we discovered the hidden compartment, I've been checking on the office periodically to make sure nothing else is out of place."

"You suspected one of her people might try to get in?"

"I'd be a fool not to."

I guess she has good reason to be paranoid. "But you didn't tell anyone else about the book."

"Obviously not."

"Still. Someone knew." If they hadn't, they wouldn't have known where to look. "I realise that you don't want to draw attention to this, but I don't even know which coven members work in this building. Have you spoken to any of them yet?"

"Yes," she said. "I asked everyone who works on this floor, but nobody confessed to going near Mina's office."

"There are a few hundred other witches who use this building, aren't there? Any of them might have dropped by in the middle of the night."

"Correct." She pursed her lips. "Wendy, you're the only witness, as far as we know. Is there anything else you think we ought to know?"

"No, I don't think so." Wendy didn't meet the coven leader's eyes, which might have been a red flag if she didn't look like she was about to pass out. "Am… am I being fired?"

"Fired?" echoed Jennifer. "Don't be absurd. I simply wanted to hear your story. You're too valuable to fire."

Wendy swayed on her feet. I wondered if I ought to put a cushion under her in case she did faint, but she recovered herself at the last moment. "I… thank you."

"You can go," added Jennifer.

As Wendy tottered out of the office, I faced the coven

leader. "We aren't going to question every single coven member, are we? Or was Wendy a special case because she was the only witness?"

"The latter," she said. "I do intend to talk to the other coven members myself, but I suspect that if an active member of the coven did steal the book, they wouldn't have been foolish enough to hide such contraband inside their office."

Are you sure about that? "You don't want me to poke around? As Wendy so nicely pointed out, I *can* walk through walls."

"No." She pursed her lips. "If necessary, I'll search the other offices myself but only if I feel that someone is lying to me."

Then why had she needed me to come here? "What about the ex-coven members? I know most of them are in jail…"

"Correct."

"Do you think any of them were involved?" I'd assumed Jennifer had asked for my help because of my own history with Mina Devlin, but so far, nothing about the theft had felt particularly relevant to me. Even her comment about me supposedly being impartial meant nothing whatsoever to the other members of the coven.

"Not directly," she replied. "And if they were, they almost certainly had the help of someone who *is* a current member. I intend to visit them later today after I've spoken to the active coven members."

"You aren't going to ask me to talk to them?"

"No, unless you want to," she said. "I know you have a ghost tour tonight. You wouldn't want to let down your guests, would you?"

"No." I was glad to see she knew where my priorities were. "I'm just a little lost as to why you picked me in the first place. Wendy had a point—I'm technically as likely a suspect as anyone else who isn't a coven member. If not more, given the 'walking through walls' thing."

"Yes, but it's obvious that you aren't the thief." A touch of impatience entered her voice. "I did make it clear why I asked you to help earlier, didn't I? You've met my predecessor and seen to the imprisonment of her allies."

"Yes, but that doesn't make me an expert on her." Or whatever dodgy books of dark magic she'd kept in her office that were apparently alluring to thieves. Honestly, this kind of situation would be less common if the witches didn't insist upon relying on magic instead of installing CCTV inside their headquarters.

"Neither are the police." Jennifer's jaw twitched. "They have no intention of questioning every coven member, nor do I expect them to, but they also can't unearth Mina's allies and make a list."

"Again, it's not like *I* have a list either." I studied her face. "Did you really want me to help you as a witch? Or as a Reaper?"

A moment passed before she answered. "Both. I understand that your half-Reaper status grants you certain… abilities to see things that are invisible to the eyes of others."

"You want me to look around Mina's office?" I guessed. "You might have led with that."

"I wanted to determine Wendy's knowledge first." She pulled out a desk drawer and retrieved a bundle of keys. "We'll look now."

"You promise the door isn't booby-trapped?"

"I'll open the door myself." She lifted the keys and jangled them. "It's quite safe."

I'll believe that when I see it. I let her lead the way out of the office and then followed her downstairs, Wendy trailing behind us like a nervous ghost. Speaking of ghosts, Mart seemed to have wandered off. Must have got bored.

"Here." Jennifer crossed the lobby to a wooden door marked with a gold-plated plaque declaring it to be Mina Devlin's office. With her wand in one hand and the key in the other, she performed a complex series of wand movements while rotating the key in the lock until the door clicked inward.

To all appearances, Mina's office looked like its owner had just stepped outside for a walk. No surprise, given that Wendy had been fastidiously cleaning the place on a daily basis. Cabinets and shelves lined the wall behind the desk, though I didn't see anything that pinged on my Reaper abilities. I *did* smell herbs—specifically, sage. Someone didn't want ghosts in here.

"It was there." Wendy pointed at a sizeable cabinet tucked into a back corner. "The thief had pushed the cabinet back into place after stealing the book."

Jennifer crossed the room and pointed her wand at the cabinet, causing it to slide away from the wall. Sure enough, a small door swung open in the back, revealing a cubbyhole.

"Was there anything else in there?" I tried to look inside, but Wendy stepped into my line of sight, nervously watching her coven leader.

"Not that I could see."

"Right." I sidestepped Wendy and peered into the cubbyhole, but nothing appeared to be in there except a large quantity of dust. "I don't see anything. What did you expect, a demonic artefact?"

Wendy let out a frightened noise and bumped into the desk with her knee, earning an eye-roll from me. Honestly, you'd think the police were about to show up and put her in handcuffs at any moment.

"It was worth a try." Jennifer returned the cabinet to its original position with a flick of her wand and then swept out of the room, beckoning Wendy and me to follow her. "I've called a coven meeting tonight to talk to the others. However, to visit Mina's allies who are currently imprisoned, I'll need to get permission from the police."

"Is that what you want me to do?" She must know I had little influence with most of the local officers, with one exception. "I can talk to Drew later, but I can't make any promises."

Granted, I wouldn't mind having another chat with Mina's jailed supporters myself in case any of them might let slip exactly who had tried to drown me in those tunnels.

Jennifer gave a tight nod. "If you will. Thanks for your time."

When I left the coven headquarters, Mart came drifting up to me. "Even *I* can't get into that office."

"I wondered where you'd gone," I remarked. "You tried to get into Mina's office?"

"The entire room is surrounded by sage," he said. "If you ask me, that assistant was the thief. Who else had the key to the door?"

"Jennifer did, but Mina's followers will certainly have known about that secret compartment." I dug my hands in my pockets as a cool autumn breeze blew overhead. "I think Jennifer's more bothered by someone undermining her authority than the actual theft."

"Did she tell you what the book actually *is*?" Mart enquired.

"A tome of illegal dark magic, apparently." It wasn't hard to imagine the sort of magic Mina had wanted to research. "I don't know any of the current coven members well enough to make a judgement call. It might be any of them who stole the book... or it might be an outsider."

"What about the ones in jail?"

"They're next on the list, assuming Drew agrees to let Jennifer come into the jail to talk to them."

"I don't see a certain officer letting *you* into the jail, let alone Jennifer."

I groaned. "Petra. Yeah, she's going to be a problem. I think she respects the coven leader more than she does me, but it's hard to tell."

"I'd be more than happy to cause a distraction," he offered. "Just give me the word."

"Not yet," I told him. "I don't *want* to go to the jail without a plan. Otherwise, I'll just get into an argument with Marie or Angela and end up hexing them." The pair of notorious gossips had been in Mina's inner circle and would find it hilarious that something had been stolen out from under the current coven leader's nose.

"You don't actually think one of them stole the book, do you?"

"No, but they might know who did," I said. "Also, I'd like to know who tried to have me drowned."

"Mina did." Mart drifted alongside me as we left the high street behind. "I don't like that Jennifer wants you to do *her* job. Doesn't she know the coven better than you do?"

"She's going to do most of the questioning herself," I said, "but I've met Mina. I know how she operates. I can also walk through walls, as Wendy so helpfully reminded me."

"She accused *you* of breaking in?" He scoffed. "I told you she was the guilty one."

"She's not Mina's ally, Mart." Not even remotely. "She's slavishly devoted to her coven leader, to the extent that she even runs around cleaning Mina's office. If she'd taken the book, she'd have run like hell, not stuck around and subjected herself to questioning."

"You'll see."

We argued back and forth for a bit longer before I remembered I'd intended to message Drew and ask him about talking to the jailed witches. I texted him as we crossed the bridge, pausing for a moment to have a look underneath. Nobody was there, not even a certain officer. *I knew she was all talk.*

When I reached the inn's entrance, Allie met me at the door. "Maura, we had a call from someone asking for you."

"Asking for me?" That was unexpected. "What, to the inn's landline?"

"Yes."

Weird. I didn't go around handing my mobile phone number to just anyone, but the inn's landline was publicly available on the Wizarding Web. That didn't mean many people knew *I* worked here, though. "Are they still on the line?"

"No, I told them you were out." She walked to the desk and picked up a piece of paper. "I did write down their number."

"All right." I took the paper from her—and a thrill of dread rippled through my nerves.

It was the landline number of the house where Mart and I had grown up.

4

Why would my dad have called the inn? I stared at the page as if the markings would rearrange themselves if I looked at them intently enough—but I knew that number like the back of my hand even after all these years.

"Maura, you look like you saw a ghost." Mart laughed loudly at his own joke. I ignored him.

"Maura?" Allie peered at my face. "What's wrong?"

"This… They shouldn't have this number." I crumpled the paper in my hand. "No way."

"Who?" Alarm flitted across her face.

"Someone from my past. Not dangerous," I amended. "I don't think so, anyway."

Reapers were dangerous by nature, of course, but why would anyone from my home have any reason to contact me here? Unless…

Unless they knew I hadn't stopped using my Reaper skills after I'd quit.

"Hey!" Mart snatched the paper from my hand, where the page hovered in the air before his widening eyes. "No way."

"Exactly." To say my dad and I hadn't parted on the best of

terms was an understatement. I'd broken the Reapers' rules in a major way when I'd stopped my brother's ghost from passing into the eternal afterworld after his untimely death, binding him to me instead. Dad might have flaunted the Reapers' rules himself when he'd married my mother and had two kids, but he drew the line at violating their most important principle. The dead were dead, no exceptions. Not even for his own family.

"Do you want to call them back?" Allie asked hesitantly.

I shook my head. "No. Definitely not."

Mart blew air onto the paper, causing it to drift towards the partly open door, but I lunged and grabbed it first. Clenching my fists, I made for the stairs. I needed to get my head together before I spoke to anyone else. It was bad enough that Allie had had to see my reaction to the latest bombshell the universe had dropped on my head.

Why now? How'd he known where to find me?

"I'd like to know how he got this number," I muttered to Mart. "Any ideas?"

"It's publicly available, obviously."

I shook my head. "How would he know where to go looking? It's not like I'm listed on the website as an employee."

Granted, I'd accompanied Carey on several ghost-hunting trips, but she didn't mention me by name in her blog posts or include me in any video footage. Of course, a certain grumpy ghost blogger *had* tried to badmouth the inn and featured images of us a few weeks ago, but I'd got those taken down, and there was no good reason for my dad to be browsing ghost-hunter blogs on the internet. He didn't even have a computer in the house, for crying out loud. Still…

I reached the door to my room and retrieved my key from my pocket. "Is there the slightest chance he might have seen a certain blogger's attempts to troll us?"

Mart scoffed. "Does Dad even know how to use the internet?"

"Even if he does, he won't know there's a whole industry of real-life ghost bloggers." The same could be said of the Reaper Council, who'd scarcely changed in the centuries of their existence. They shunned all mortal conveniences, including the Wizarding Web, but they didn't need to use a search engine to find anyone—and I'd been counting on them *not* wanting to find me. As an ex-Reaper who didn't draw attention to herself, I should have been far down on their priority list.

My dad, though? There was nothing stopping him from stepping through the afterworld and crashing straight into my new life with the force of a boulder rolling down a mountainside.

I unlocked the door, entered my room, and let out a groan. "What the *hell* am I supposed to do? Call him back?"

"Nope," Mart said. "If he wanted you to come home, he'd have visited here in person, not called the inn's landline."

"Yeah." I was under no illusions there. Dad was a full Reaper, not a half Reaper like me, and if he'd wanted me at his side, there wasn't anything I could have done to stop him from marching in here and forcibly dragging me home.

Not that he would. He did have *some* sense of compassion towards his one surviving child, and he'd already stood back as I left my hometown and threw my Reaper apprenticeship out the window. He of all people knew there was no point in training an unwilling Reaper, but that hadn't been why I'd left.

Mart drifted around the room, stirring up a breeze that raised goose bumps on my arms. "Why him? I'd have expected Mum to call us first."

"Yeah." The pair were amicably separated—mostly because the Reaper's rules forbade attachments to mortals, and my dad's moment of weakness in seeking a relationship with my mother was a constant source of irritation to the Reaper Council—but they still spoke to one another. "If she had, she'd have stayed on the line until I got back to the inn and probably told Allie our entire sob story in the process."

Reapers and witches were chalk and cheese. Dad was ever the stoic Reaper. Mum was more of the emotional sort whose habit of calling to beg me to come home had grated on me so much that I'd ended up changing my phone number just to shake her off. Not the most mature way of handling the situation, but I'd been eighteen when I'd left town, raw with grief from losing my twin brother.

Now... Well, I wouldn't say my reaction to Dad's phone call had been particularly mature, either, but the shock had hit too hard for me to make a rational decision. Sure, the quickest way to find out what Dad wanted was to call him back, but all my instincts screamed against it. I had quite enough problems to handle without the ghosts of my past showing up again.

The sound of Mart turning on the shower reached my ears. "Please don't flood the place. We have a tour in a few hours."

"Exactly," he called back.

Honestly. At least my brother didn't have to be the one to make the final decision on whether to return our dad's call. As for me? If I stayed up here too long, the others would either get suspicious or think I was in trouble.

If I used my mobile phone, my number would be around half my hometown by morning. Using the inn's landline came with the risk of someone overhearing, but I'd already had to buy a new phone a few weeks ago after my impromptu swim in the river. With the landline, I wouldn't need to switch numbers again to shake off unwanted family members.

I listened to the sound of water pounding on the shower floor for a long moment before asking my brother, "What should I tell him?"

"You're going to call him back?" The running water ceased, and my brother reappeared from the bathroom, arms folded across his transparent chest.

"It's that or risk him calling the inn again while we're in the middle of the tour," I replied. "I'm not going to let that happen."

"Borrow Drew's phone, then."

"He's still at work." And I didn't want to drag him into this either. "I'll use the landline, but... what do I even say?"

"Tell him he's got the wrong number for pizza delivery."

"Very funny." Giving up on getting any sense out of my brother, I made for the door. Mart didn't follow me. No doubt he disagreed with my decision, which I'd expected, though I hoped he wouldn't flood my room in protest.

I closed the door behind me and headed for the stairs, figuring it was better to get the call over with than spend the whole ghost tour brooding.

As I reached the foot of the stairs, Carey came bounding over to me. "I wondered where you'd gone, Maura."

"Sorry," I said. "Mart's in a mood. I have to make a quick call, and then we can plan tonight's tour, okay?"

"What call?"

"Something came up." I fixed a smile on my face and approached her mother at the reception desk. "Allie, is it all right if I borrow the phone for a bit?"

"Of course." She looked a little worried—no doubt I hadn't sounded as calm as I'd intended—but she nodded. "You can use the phone in the back room if you want some privacy."

"Cheers." I walked into the little-used small room behind the front desk where she kept the inn's paperwork then waited to make sure nobody was within hearing distance before making the call. My pulse thrummed in my fingertips. *Here we go.*

I dialled the number and held my breath, listening to the familiar shrill ringing noise on the other end. My mum might have upgraded to a mobile phone in recent years, but my dad still used the same old landline he'd had since before I was born. Better than most Reapers, who didn't bother with such mundane conveniences that allowed other people to contact them, but hardly high-tech.

The ringing stopped, and a cold, terse voice spoke. "Yes?"

"Dad." I gripped the phone, my palm sweaty. "It's me."

"Maura."

"Yeah." I swallowed against my dry throat. "I don't suppose you'd like to tell me how you got this number?"

"Shelton."

"What?" I nearly dropped the phone. *"Him?"*

That Reaper. Shelton had shown up in town for the purposes of hunting down an escaped hellbeast a few months before and had instantly become suspicious of me, assuming I was a Reaper operating outside of the council's rules. In fairness, I'd been suspicious of him, too, but he'd turned out to be helping old Harold, the local Reaper. I'd never have believed he would contact my family. *Why would he do that?*

"Him," Dad agreed. "He informed me that you were working at a place called the Riverside Inn. It wasn't hard to find the details."

That wasn't a good sign. "And... why did you want to call me?"

I might have asked what else Shelton had told him—such as the fact that Hawkwood Hollow was full of ghosts and a grumpy old Reaper who refused to do his job—but surely he wouldn't have broken his promise so easily. Would he?

"Do I need a reason to get in touch with my daughter?"

"As a Reaper, yes. I thought you shunned all human attachments." I'd also thought he'd have made more of an effort to find me before now. Sure, I'd kept my distance, but he was my dad, after all.

"Don't be absurd," he said. "You're my child. You're also skirting the line of the Reaper Council's laws, I'm told."

Here we go. "Who told you that, Shelton? Did he also mention that I saved his life?"

"You didn't have to leave all of this behind, you know."

"What?" Where had that come from? "You told me eight years ago that once I made my choice, that was it. No going back."

"I may have spoken in haste," he said. "My son was dead. You…"

I raised him from the dead and bound him to me. How could he rip the wounds open after all these years? "You made your stance clear." He had, and I'd never forgotten. "You're years too late. I'm not going to uproot myself and come running home now."

"Are you really so attached to that inn?" he asked. "Running ghost tours is beneath you."

"Excuse me?" My voice went cold. "You don't know anything about my life. I'm happy here. Much happier than I'd be stalking dead souls. If you want an apprentice, go and find someone else."

"I'm not looking for an apprentice." He sounded rather put out. "It just occurred to me—"

"For what reason?" Beneath the cocktail of anger and resentment, suspicion stirred. "Why did Shelton get in touch with you in the first place?"

"Reapers talk to each other."

"No, they don't. You're notorious loners."

"Sometimes we talk to each other," he corrected. "You

know that. I just wanted to ask if you were willing to come back home so we can have a face-to-face discussion."

"You have got to be kidding me." I did my level best to keep my voice Reaper-cold and not let my anger slip in. "What in hell brought this on? Don't lie to me. You can't have had a change of heart out of nowhere."

"You don't believe me?" He sounded more resigned than surprised. "I'll give you time to think about your decision. I know this came as a shock."

"You don't say." Anger crept into my voice. "Sorry to disappoint you, but I'm not giving up my job or my home. Did you want to talk to Mart too?"

His breath hitched, and an instant later, the phone call ended.

"Guess not, then," I muttered to the dial tone.

I should have known my words would hit a sore spot, but when I put the phone down, I was alarmed to find my own cheeks wet with tears. Furious, I scrubbed my face with the back of my sleeve. So much for playing the stoic Reaper.

"Maura?" Jia called to me from near the front desk. "Something wrong?"

"Nothing." I took in a breath and stepped out to join her. "I'm having a… weird day. Is Carey at the bar?"

"Allie is." Her forehead creased in concern. "Maura, if there's anything you need help with, I'm here. Any bodies you need me to bury, I'll get the shovel."

My eyes burned. Dammit. "No, that's not necessary. Reapers are kinda hard to bury."

I was tired of keeping secrets, and I could do worse than let Jia in on this one. She was the least likely to judge.

"Reapers?" Her mouth parted. "You were talking to *them?*"

"My dad," I amended. "He decided to contact me for the first time in eight years and asked me to join the Reapers again. I said no, but if I'm a bit spaced-out during the tour, that's why."

"No, I don't blame you." She sucked in a breath. "I haven't spoken to my dad in years either. Yours is a full Reaper?"

"Hence the lack of contact after I broke all their rules and quit my apprenticeship."

"Wow." Jia glanced over at the transparent doors to the restaurant, which was beginning to swell with the evening crowd. "Allie wants my help in there. Tell me the rest later?"

"No, I'll come too," I said. "I need a distraction—though I should probably make sure Mart hasn't flooded my room first."

"Not again." She pursed her lips. "Did he not take the news well?"

"Definitely not," I said. "He's the reason I left home. Dad never acknowledged my brother as an actual person after I brought him back."

"Harsh."

"That's a Reaper for you." I heaved a sigh. "I haven't the faintest idea what brought this on, but I'll check on my brother, and then I'll come back to work."

I wasn't in the right frame of mind to deal with customers *or* plan ghost tours, but at least my job mostly involved standing behind the crowd and watching for trouble. Mart was part of the main event, but the others were used to weirdness from him by now.

My phone buzzed on the way upstairs, yanking me back to reality. A message from Drew. *Sorry, something came up at work—I'll come over at the end of the tour?*

Typical. I replied and said that was fine then entered my room. Inside, the bathroom door remained closed. "Mart?"

"Go away."

"Don't you want to know what Dad said?" I sat down on

the bed. "Shelton visited him and blabbed about us. That was how he found out."

"I knew I didn't like that guy." He drifted back out of the bathroom, a scowl on his ghostly face. "What does he want?"

"He asked me to resume my Reaper training."

Mart collapsed into peals of laughter. The sound was more of a half-wailing, half-groaning noise, and when the door started to rattle, I pressed my hands to my ears. "Mart, cut that out. Save the dramatics for the ghost tour."

The noise stopped. "Resume your training? What planet has he been on?"

"One where the past eight years never happened, apparently." I flopped over backwards on the bed, tempted to have a nap on the off chance that I'd wake up in a few hours and the world would make sense again. "I don't get it either. He wouldn't say why he had this change of heart."

"Unless the council came snooping."

"Why would they?" I lifted my head. "They'd have come here first rather than telling tales on me to my dad."

"I don't know. Your name is out there," he said. "With the Wardens, with the ghost-blogger community…"

"The Reapers don't go around looking up ghost-tour blogs. You know that." The Wardens, though? Maybe someone had mentioned my name, but I'd trusted them. Why would they have reported me to the Reaper Council?

"They look for rogues." He flipped over in midair. "They also look for practitioners of illegal magic. You know they'd be all over Mina Devlin if they realised what she was doing in that tunnel."

"Twenty years ago." I sat bolt upright. "Crap. Is this *her*, do you think? She can't have figured out where I lived."

"She'd have good reason to try."

"Yes." She would, but it would also have taken a hell of a lot of detective work for someone to trace me back to my old town. There weren't too many half Reapers out there in the world, but the council were cagey with their information, and they didn't store it online where the public could access it either.

No, I wasn't convinced, but just the thought of Mina having found out where I'd grown up had my mind spinning in circles. Had my dad contacted me out of a sudden surge of regret for our past arguments… or was there a more sinister reason?

5

I had no idea how I got through the ghost tour that night. Mart was subdued, too, though his ghostly antics remained exciting enough not to make our guests suspicious. They especially got a kick out of his new-to-them habit of wandering around with an inflatable pumpkin bobbing on his ghostly head.

As for the other ghosts, they were good enough at their routines not to need too much supervision. Vicky, the youngest, had adopted her own floating pumpkin to wear on her head while she skipped around grabbing people's hands when they weren't expecting it. Jonathan made shadows appear on the walls, morphing them into pumpkins and bats and other Halloween-themed shapes. Brian contributed by chilling the air and freezing the windows, while middle-aged couple Wade and Louise had a double act in which they opened and closed doors, rattled windows, and flickered lights on and off in time to creepy music.

In truth, it was one of our better nights, and yet my heart just wasn't in it. My background role meant nobody noticed except for Jia, who at least understood the reason for my sour mood. I did have other excuses lined up, such as the witches' attempts to manipulate me into finding a thief for them. I'd given Carey a brief explanation of Jennifer's unexpected request earlier, but I could tell she wasn't quite satisfied with my insistence that I was holding the witches at arm's length and letting them deal with the actual thief-catching themselves.

It was a relief when I checked my phone and found a message from Drew saying he was on his way to the inn. As the guests went into the restaurant for Carey's final speech of the night, I hung back in the lobby to wait for him. Without the crowd of guests, the cold breeze from outside was more evident, and I stood out of range of the automatic doors to keep what little warmth remained inside.

When the doors slid open, I moved closer to look for Drew, but he wasn't there. Neither was anyone else, but the doors opened as if an invisible figure stood just outside.

"Who's there?" I stepped out, drawing my arms around my chest in a futile effort to keep out the chill. Maybe it'd been a ghost, but they didn't usually have enough presence to cause motion sensors to respond.

A faint stirring of shadows drew my gaze to the bushes across from the inn's entrance, near the river. I headed in that direction and then spied a figure on the bridge. This time it was definitely Drew, and an unexpected rush of emotion hit me at the sight of him. Before I'd quite got a grip on my senses, I ran over and wrapped him in a hug.

He stiffened in surprise then hugged me back. "Maura. What're you doing out here? I'd have thought you'd be staying out of the cold."

"I thought I saw someone outside. Might've been a ghost."

"Really?" He followed my gaze to the bushes growing along the riverbank. "With your track record, Maura?"

"Fair point." I released him, scanning the bushes myself. "I don't know. Ghosts can't usually trigger the motion sensors on the doors, but I guess a bird might have landed outside."

Drew made a sceptical noise, and I found my attention travelling down the dark riverbank towards the curved underside of the bridge. When I peered around to see better into the darkness, Drew gently took hold of my arm. "Don't walk into the river, Maura."

"Wasn't my plan."

"You did it once already."

"You weren't with me that time."

"So the solution is for me to be with you at all times?"

"Ha." I craned my neck, but there might have been a whole family of ghouls down there, and I wouldn't have been able to see them in the dark. "No, the solution is to send a team of officers down there to have a proper look around when the tunnels are clear."

"Funnily enough, you aren't the first person to propose that idea," he said. "I had an unusual call from the coven leader earlier."

"She called you?" I twisted around to peer at his face. "Wow, she really meant it?"

"I assume that was what you wanted to talk to me about?"

"Right. Yeah." I'd implied I wanted to have a serious discussion when I'd texted him earlier, but I'd been referencing my dad's bizarre phone call. Honestly, I'd forgotten to check if Jennifer had made any headway with the police. "Jennifer and I agreed that if I helped her find this thief, she'd try to escalate the investigation into those tunnels to keep certain officers from whining at me."

"Nice of her," he commented. "*Did* you find the thief?"

"Not yet." I turned my back on the river. "She asked me to question Wendy of all people, but then she said I probably wouldn't be interested in watching her talk to everyone else in the coven, which is true enough. There's no way they'd spill their secrets in front of me."

"That's true." His gaze lingered on the bridge. "If you think you did see someone earlier, I can make a call."

"No." I shook my head. "Never mind. It's probably nothing."

"You're not usually so quick to dismiss something that's bugging you."

"Everything is bugging me." I returned my attention to the inn, where the guests had begun to disperse through the front doors, to avoid catching his eye.

"Really." He was silent for a moment. "I thought the tunnels were at the top of your priority list."

"They are." I shrugged one shoulder. "But my quickest route to answers is through Jennifer, and I doubt her thief is hiding down there in the damp and cold."

"You never know," he said. "Does she have any other suspects aside from Wendy?"

I began to walk away from the river, back towards the inn. "She also wanted to talk to Mina's jailed allies. I'm guessing she told you that on the phone too?"

"She did," he said. "She can't possibly think one of them committed robbery from inside jail, can she?"

"No, but they might have an idea of Mina's current movements," I replied. "Did you give her permission?"

"I said I'd see what I could do." He tilted his head. "You want to talk to them too?"

"About as much as I want to swim in the river," I said. "But… yes. I think they're more likely to know what Mina's doing than anyone else."

"I doubt they'll be cooperative, but if it's what you want, I can take you there tomorrow."

"Thanks." It was like thanking him for booking me a

dental appointment, but it had to be done. "Ah—have you mentioned any of this to Petra?"

"No, because she isn't in charge," he said. "I'm not planning to pick her for the team I'll send into the tunnels either."

"It might shut her up," I said. "She doesn't tend to believe anything she can't see with her own eyes."

"That's true." He stepped around a young couple dressed in pumpkin-patterned clothes who were leaving the inn, swaying a little as a result of too many cocktails. "But Maura… It's possible that the water levels will never be low enough to safely explore."

"There's another entrance," I pointed out. "And Mina's allies wouldn't let a little water stop them using the tunnels to sneak into town if they could get away with it."

"Yes. I'll have to cordon off that entrance." He stopped talking as we walked past a group of guests on the way into the inn who stared at both of us with awed expressions. Whispers trailed behind us.

"That's the Reaper."

"Why isn't she in costume?"

"Right, why isn't she?"

I bit back a snarky comment about the local costume shop being out of inflatable scythes and entered the lobby before I accidentally caused a scene. Some of the guests were leaving to return home, others were traipsing back to their rooms, and still more were pestering Carey with questions concerning our local ghosts and our Halloween plans. My head throbbed at the assault of noise, and I wished there was a secret staircase so we could get upstairs without running into anyone else.

"There you are," said Jia, catching sight of me. "Hey, Drew."

"Hey." I dropped my voice. "I need an early night. Can you tell Carey?"

"Sure thing." Worry flickered in her eyes. "Are you all right?"

"Yes, but if one more person wonders why I'm not wearing a Reaper costume, there's going to be an incident."

"Uh-oh." Jia eyed the stairway. "Drew, can you shield Maura from the mob?"

"Already there." Drew swept ahead of me to the staircase, his intimidating air of authority effectively clearing the path without any resistance. I followed, doing my best to impersonate a shadow, until we reached the door to my room.

Once inside, I dropped my fake smile with relief and then groaned when I spied water trickling from under my bathroom door. "Mart, *really*."

"Your brother's up to his usual tricks, is he?" Drew asked. "I thought he was helping with the tour."

"He is. I just didn't notice this earlier." I pulled out my wand to clean up the mess. "He's in a mood."

"So are you," he pointed out. "Is this about the coven? Or the tunnels?"

"It's been a long day." I didn't want to lie to him, but frankly, I didn't even know where to begin with the latest development. Drew didn't know much about my history before I'd come to Hawkwood Hollow. He hadn't pried, and that alone made me want to trust him with the truth. "Something else happened earlier."

"What?" He sat on the edge of the bed, his gaze following my movements while I paced around the room. "What is it?"

"I had a call." I sat next to him, my gaze on the ceiling. "From... my old home. My dad."

"Your dad?" Surprise filled his voice. "Is he...?"

"A Reaper. Yes." I lowered my head to look directly at him, but he looked more puzzled than anything else. "He wasn't thrilled with me for ditching my apprenticeship, so we haven't spoken in years. Let's just say I wasn't expecting him to have a change of heart and call the inn to invite me to come home."

"That seems… odd." His brow furrowed. "You did turn him down, right?"

"Of course I did." I leaned my head against Drew's shoulder, taking comfort from his closeness. "He also claimed that Shelton was the one who told him where I was, which seems equally weird."

"Him?" Drew asked. "He wasn't part of the Reaper Council?"

"No, and my dad isn't either," I said. "They sort of frown upon relationships with humans, let alone having two kids with one. Dad's a rule-follower to the core, though, and to say he disapproves of my general life choices is an understatement."

"What about your mother?"

"I don't know if he told her." I shrugged. "They split up years ago. A coven leader and a Reaper were never going to last. He's immortal, and she isn't, for a start. My brother's death was the final nail in that coffin. Literally."

"Immortal?" Wariness entered his voice. "You aren't, right? I'm sure you told me…"

"I wouldn't easily be able to shake off the Reapers if I was," I said. "Given that I broke the rules myself when I bound my brother's ghost to me, I'm not exactly welcome among them. My dad made that clear when I left."

"Now he's in touch again?"

"Apparently so." The call had brought back a flurry of mixed feelings, but one thing was certain: I had no intention of giving up my new life. "He hung up on me when I asked if he wanted to talk to my brother, so that might be the end of it, but… I don't know."

"That's rough." He wrapped his arm around my shoulder. "If you wanted to check, I'm pretty sure the Reaper

Council wouldn't object to you visiting family, would they?"

"They wouldn't know or care, but I don't need to be dragged into old drama." I leaned into his embrace. "If I showed up at my dad's house, my mum would find out and try to guilt-trip me into staying. I'm not sure if he told her what Shelton said, but this isn't exactly a good time for everyone from my old life to start barging into my business."

"I bet." He ran a hand through my hair. "Honestly, in your place, I'd let it go. Wait for him to call back if he wants."

"That's the plan, but…" A thought remained lodged at the back of my mind. Namely, Mart's suspicion that there was a reason Shelton had given my dad the means of contacting me again. "This is all convoluted, and I'm not sure who's involved, but Mart thought a certain ex-coven leader might have tried something."

Drew released me. "What, he thinks she's poking into your old life?"

"She might be trying to, but Dad's an actual Reaper. You could push him off a cliff and he'd walk away unscathed. An ex-coven leader wouldn't intimidate him in the least."

"I imagine not," he said. "Still, like I said, I wouldn't object if you wanted to visit home. I could even come with you for moral support."

I shuddered. "Thanks for the offer, but I swore never to set foot in that place again."

If I had to break that promise, I wouldn't object to having him by my side, but that would have to stay in the "last resort" category.

"I don't blame you." He planted a kiss on my mouth. "Is there anything I can do to help?"

"This helps." I kissed him back. "Honestly—I'd rather be here. I made my choice, and I picked Hawkwood Hollow. This is my home."

But would that be enough to stand against the weight of my past?

———

The following morning, I accompanied Drew to work. He'd agreed to pull some strings to get me into the jail to talk to the imprisoned witches and ask some questions—but he'd been somewhat hindered by the fact that Jennifer had walked in there at the crack of dawn and demanded to speak to the prisoners.

"Seriously?" I asked when he broke the news after receiving a call from the terrified receptionist at the police station. "All this fuss about her needing my help, and then she goes and talks to the witches without me. Why did nobody stop her?"

"I assume whoever was working in the jail this morning was too intimidated to turn the coven leader away." He didn't sound thrilled, but it was a tad too late to evict her at this point.

"If it was Petra, I'm not going to be impressed." I'd already dragged myself out of bed, so I decided to walk with him to the jail anyway to find out just what kind of chaos Jennifer had unleashed.

No sign remained of the coven leader in the police-station lobby, though the usually grumpy werewolf recep-tionist descended on Drew with hand-wringing apologies worthy of Wendy. Drew shook her off with the promise that he'd be back once he'd determined that nothing was amiss inside the jail itself, and he led me through the adjacent door to the prison cells. One perk of Jennifer's unexpected visit was that nobody looked twice at me, and we walked past the holding cells housing short-term prisoners without drawing too much attention.

Through another door, we found ourselves in the main part of the jail, and I found my attention drawn to a cell in which a middle-aged witch sat reading a book. *Oh, right. I forgot about her.*

Debora Rowe, former librarian and summoner of monsters, put down the book and gave me a mocking smile. "Reaper. What a pleasant surprise."

I guess I'm starting with you, then. "Heard from your former coven leader lately?"

"What do you think?" she asked. "I've scarcely seen anyone outside of this miserable place. Now I get two visitors in one day."

"You did encourage a bunch of teenagers to summon monsters from the afterworld, if you've forgotten," I said. "You earned your place here."

Her jaw twitched. "You can't stay out of the coven's business, can you?"

"Hey, it was Jennifer who asked me to help her this time." I hoped that detail might shock her into giving something away. "How close were you to Mina?"

She'd pretended to be a mild-mannered librarian up until the moment I'd exposed her as having convinced a bunch of teenagers to summon ghost-eating monsters. Her aim had been to drive me out of town and prevent me from poking into the past, which no doubt included a certain set of tunnels too.

When Debora said nothing, Drew spoke from behind me. "You were a librarian. Did you know Mina possessed a certain volume of dark magic in her office?"

Did Jennifer tell him that? She must have mentioned it on the phone; I hadn't had time to get into the details with the distraction of my unexpected call from home.

Debora still gave no answer, and I moved closer to the barred door of her cell. "You aren't going anywhere, you know. Are you scared Mina will come in here and curse you if you tell us anything?"

"She won't." She lifted her head to meet my eyes. "You should have left this town alone. That was all I wanted. Remember that when the Reaper Council comes for you."

Tension zipped up my spine. "What makes you so sure they will?"

Maybe it was because yesterday's phone call was still raw in my memory, but her words put me in mind of my dad's words when I'd left home—that some things were unforgivable, at least in the eyes of the Reaper Council.

"I think you know, Reaper. Not everything can stay buried forever."

Buried. In the tunnels. "Did *you* know someone was using a secret tunnel to practise illegal magic?"

"Would it matter if I did?"

Yes... and no. I'd already figured out that Mina's allies had been aware of the tunnels without needing to question them, but until I got concrete proof of what they'd been using the tunnels for, I wouldn't have any new evidence to use against them.

"It might," I began, "if the people using that tunnel committed a crime worse than simply summoning a few monsters. What do you think of that?"

Debora gave a short laugh. "I think you're in over your head, Reaper."

She picked up her book again, indicating that the conversation was over. *Great.* Had she shared anything else with Jennifer? I toyed with the idea of using my Reaper abilities to hop into her cell and scare the crap out of her, but Drew placed a hand on my shoulder and spoke in a low voice. "Want to talk to anyone else? I can't give you more than a few minutes in here."

"Right." I dragged my attention away from the librarian

and spied another familiar face behind the bars of another cell. Marie. The middle-aged witch wore a sullen expression that became a glare when she spied me watching her.

"Don't bother, Reaper," she growled at me. "I've had my fill of inane questions. It's not my problem if our sorry excuse for a coven leader managed to get robbed underneath her own nose."

Did Jennifer tell her? It wasn't impossible to read between the lines, but I didn't like how smug Mina's followers were acting, as if I were the one behind bars and not them.

"Maybe that isn't what I want to ask about." I crossed the corridor to her cell. "Did Mina entrust one of you with redoing the spells concealing the tunnels under the bridge?"

Marie gave a laugh, which was echoed by the person in the cell on her left-hand side—Angela.

"What?" I said, irked. "It's not hard to guess that Mina had you running there to put spells on that would hide the place from prying eyes."

"You don't need to ask such obvious questions, dear," Angela snickered. "We already think you're clueless."

"I was trying to work out which of you tried to drown me so I can return the favour." I let a smidgeon of creepiness enter my voice and shadows cloak my hands, but with Drew at my side, I didn't quite dare push any further. "Well?"

"Not all of us can walk through walls, sweetheart," said Marie, no longer laughing. "Focus on your thief instead."

"Oh, I am." I let the shadows increase in volume so that I looked like I was wearing a dark cloak. "I'm guessing you were aware of the hidden cubbyhole in Mina's office?"

"Tiresome." Angela gave a slight laugh, but she edged to the back of her cell to get away from my shadowy hands. "I heard the coven leader had another break-in last night. Perhaps you should talk to her instead."

Did she now?

"Maura." Drew's voice yanked me back to earth. With reluctance, I let go of the shadows cloaking my hands.

"Fine." I turned my back on Mina's allies. "Forget this."

"Wise idea." He gave the witches a distrustful look as we walked past the cells and left them behind. "What now?"

"I think I should talk to the coven leader again." I spoke in a low voice. "Another break-in? I wonder if anything else was stolen?"

Even if it hadn't been, Jennifer had given away more than she'd likely intended when she'd gone to the jail. I'd thought she was more clear-headed than that, but speaking to Mina's former followers right after a second robbery in two days was bound to have gotten under her skin, especially if they'd been as smug with her as they had with me.

I hope she knows what she's doing.

6

Drew walked me to the witches' headquarters, and we parted ways outside. He added that he'd stop by the inn to say hi later, which would be my chance to update him —not only on the situation with the witches but also if I got any more unexpected phone calls from home.

Honestly, I didn't think Dad would try calling again anytime soon. I'd already said no, after all, and he knew better than to beat a metaphorical dead horse.

Unusually, Wendy didn't greet me at the door to the witches' headquarters or pursue me upstairs. When I entered Jennifer's office, I found the coven leader sat alone at the desk. "Where's your assistant?"

She eyed me calmly as I closed the door. "She decided to take a couple of days off for her mental health, at my suggestion."

"Okay." Did that mean Jennifer had frightened her off, or had she genuinely been concerned for Wendy? "I just dropped by the jail."

"Oh?" She cocked a brow. "Were the prisoners any more cooperative than they were with me?"

"Nope," I said. "What made you decide to go there first thing in the morning?"

"Didn't the police tell you?" She drummed her fingertips on the desk. "Someone broke into Mina's office again last night."

"Did they steal something else?" Right. Drew had told me, but if there'd been a second top-secret tome of illegal magic, it'd have been nice if someone had clued me in earlier.

"They didn't take anything this time," she said. "They left the door open, though, so there was no doubt that they got in."

"Weird." Was it the same thief, intending to taunt the coven leader? Or someone else playing a prank? For all we knew, they *had* taken something or other from the office that nobody had discovered yet. "Did they go into any of the other rooms?"

"Possibly the storeroom."

"The storeroom?" Had they been raiding the potion supplies?

"Everything that could be potentially dangerous has been moved," she added, as if she'd picked up on the direction of my thoughts. "The storeroom currently contains basic supplies that anyone can buy at the apothecary. Nothing that can be used in illegal spells."

"Simple herbs can be dangerous in the wrong hands."

"Yes, but it's not quite as egregious as breaking into a locked room, wouldn't you agree?" she said. "Especially a room that can only be opened by a key that I keep in my own office. The alternative, of course, is that Mina had a spare key."

"She's not here, is she?" My shoulders tensed. "In person?"

"She'd be a fool to get so close," said Jennifer. "With so many people looking for her, showing up would be more likely to backfire in her face than not. That said, I'd like to stop these break-ins before they cause people to lose faith in my ability to control my own coven members."

"Fair enough." I waited for her response, unsure why she was looking intently at me. "What's the plan, then?"

"I'd like to take them by surprise if they try the same a third time," she said. "They'll be expecting me to ambush them, no doubt, but they might not be expecting a Reaper."

"You want me to play security guard?" She had to be joking. "Not only is it not my job, but certain members of the local police think I'm intruding on their territory already. Why not ask *them* to stand on security duty if you're worried about thieves?"

"Their skills aren't what I'm looking for."

"Neither are mine." I had to make that clear. "Anyone can hide using magic. Including you."

"I intend to wait upstairs in my office," she said, "but they'll be looking out for magic. You can hide in the shadows, can't you?"

Yes, but so can any witch who uses an unseen spell. Then again, unseen spells were easy to see through for any other experienced witch or wizard and even some nonwitches. Reaper magic, though…

I shook off the thought. "Yeah, no. This is way outside of my line of work."

My own reluctance to stay in the coven headquarters all night aside, Drew would put his foot down at the mere suggestion. Besides, the break-in attempts plainly had nothing whatsoever to do with the afterworld, given the sage that had been placed around the office.

"I see." The merest hint of disappointment entered her voice. "Understandable, but I thought I'd ask."

"Can't you set up a booby trap or something?" I thought of the spell that had given me an electric shock when I'd tried to open the door to the headquarters once a while back.

"I did," she said. "The thief removed all defensive measures. We're looking at someone who has some level of skill but who won't be prepared for a nonwitch."

"Why not ask a shifter instead?" I changed tack. "Half the police are shifters. Including their chief."

"Shifters aren't known for stealth," she said. "I'm not asking you to risk your life. I thought sneaking around at night was something you often did voluntarily."

Yeah... and at one time I might have decided to hunt down the thief without being asked, but at this rate, she'd have me running errands for her next. "What if it's not the same person who stole the book?"

"Oh, it is," she said grimly. "They moved the cabinet again. Luckily, there weren't any more books in there for them to steal."

"There were plenty of books in the office." I gave her a pointed look. "What exactly is so dangerous about that one?"

"Haven't you guessed?" Weariness entered her tone. "It's a tome instructing the user in the art of necromancy. I can't say I know for sure how extensively my predecessor used it in the past, but I'm sure you can imagine the sort of magic it contains."

Necromancy. "I thought she knew how to use necromancy without the need for an instruction manual."

Hadn't Mina's followers summoned demons already? Sure, the idea of more of her followers learning wasn't exactly appealing, but I'd kind of assumed she'd already taught them.

"I thought you Reapers were educated on these things," she said. "Certain rituals require too much precision to risk attempting without the instruction manual."

"Rituals." Just how advanced was this book? "Where'd she get hold of the book to begin with? Did she steal it from a Reaper?"

"She might well have." I saw the genuine fear beneath her usually impeccable composure. Had she even slept the night before? "I'm starting to understand that I knew very little of my predecessor while she was in power."

"You aren't the only one." Yet something struck me as off. "Why not tell me earlier? If Mina had books that would tell her how to summon demons and worse, it'd be useful to know."

"I told the Reaper."

My mouth parted. "You told him and not me? What did old Harold have to say, then?"

"Harold, as expected, had no interest in looking after the book himself. He told me to keep it hidden in the office."

"Of course he did." The old Reaper had no intention of exerting himself in any way possible, not even to confiscate a book that shouldn't have been in the hands of a witch in the first place. "Let me get this straight. You're only bringing me into this now that someone's stolen it, which wouldn't have happened if you'd handed it over to the authorities."

"I thought you and the Reaper Council weren't on the best of terms."

"We aren't on *any* terms. We've barely spoken." They were the eternal bogeymen in my life, but aside from my phone call with Dad, I'd done nothing that might have drawn their attention.

But had Mina?

"I won't apologise for keeping the book hidden," she said, "but now we have a problem on our hands. The Reaper made it quite clear that if anyone got hold of Mina's book, we'd have a crisis the likes of which hasn't been seen here in twenty years."

Twenty years. The number rang in my skull, along with the certainty that the Reaper who'd spoken those words had known exactly what comparison he was drawing. Jennifer might not know the full details of the floods, but Harold did.

My nails bit into my palms. "You don't know what you're asking. If you put me in charge of catching this thief, it's my neck on the line. Besides, the police won't be thrilled at me for doing their job for them."

"I made it clear earlier that I intended to take matters into my own hands," Jennifer said. "If you catch the thief, I'll take over from there."

"I'll still have to check with Drew. I'm sure he'll have opinions." Granted, the idea of a fight was appealing after weeks of frustration over not being able to access the tunnels —but what if the thief turned out to be more than a witch or wizard?

"I understand," she said. "You can give me your answer by this evening, can't you? The sooner we catch this thief, the better for everyone."

We'll see. I wanted to have words with the Reaper, too, come to that. "I'll let you know, but I can't make any promises."

As I left the witches' headquarters, I reflected that Jennifer would have been better off asking Wendy to play security guard instead. Did she still not trust her assistant? I really couldn't tell, but it grated on my nerves that she'd told Harold, of all people, about the book and not me.

My knock on the Reaper's cottage door went unanswered. I waited ten minutes before it started to rain, and I realised I'd end up running late for my shift at the inn if I wasn't careful. Giving up for the time being, I pulled my hood over my forehead against the drizzle and walked back to the inn.

I found Mart upstairs in my room. "How're the witches?"

"Frustrating." I removed my wet coat and used my wand to dry it off. "Now they want me to play security guard."

"Where? Not in those creepy tunnels again."

"Nah, at the witches' headquarters," I said. "Jennifer said the thief came back and taunted her by leaving Mina's office door ajar, so she wants me to show up tonight and take them by surprise."

"That's not your job."

"Nope, but if one of Mina's allies is in town, it's definitely my problem." I attempted to fix my hair in the mirror. "Also, the Reaper allegedly told her that if anyone got hold of that book, they'd be able to do worse than the floods."

"And they didn't tell you?" Mart made a rude noise.

"I know. I'm not happy either." I heaved a sigh. "But Harold wouldn't have risked exposing the truth to her if he didn't genuinely think that book was dangerous. And Jennifer… When I asked if Mina stole the book from a Reaper, she said it was a distinct possibility."

"That makes it their problem, not ours."

"Mart, come on." I propped a hand on my hip. "I don't need to spell out how this could come back and bite us, do I? I don't *want* to sit in the coven's headquarters watching for thieves all night, but we don't need Mina getting her hands on even more dodgy ritualistic magic."

"I don't want to either," he said. "That was going to be your next question, wasn't it? You want me to help."

"You like wandering around outside at night anyway," I pointed out. "You also don't need to sleep."

He pulled a face. "I don't like the witches. Your coven leader trapped me in a circle of sage once, remember?"

"I remember." I should have guessed he wouldn't go for my idea. "Never mind. I'll ask another ghost."

"Now hang on a minute." Mart crossed his arms. "I didn't say I wouldn't help. Does she think the thief might be the same person who tried to drown you?"

"I didn't ask, but it's not unlikely," I replied. "We never caught them, so it's possible they're still around."

"Or it's Mina." Mart snickered to himself. "It'd be funny if we ambushed her in her own office and scared the crap out of her."

"Would she be skulking around town without showing her face to me, though?" I queried. "Nah, it's not her, but it'll be easy enough to catch the thief if we team up. You're harder to spot than I am, so if you hide in the coven headquarters, you can come back and grab me when you have the intruder, and I'll hop straight there. I'm more likely to be able to take them by surprise if I go through the afterworld."

"Why does it have to be you, though?" he asked. "Does Jennifer think you're her employee?"

"Believe me, I'm wondering the same thing myself." I left my room and locked the door behind me. "I figured even Drew wouldn't object if I didn't hide in the coven headquarters myself, and it's less hazardous than the tunnels besides."

"If I spend all night waiting for a thief who never shows up, you'll owe me."

"I know, I know."

I went downstairs to join Jia for my shift, and the rest of the day passed much as usual. Jia and I pitched our Halloween-themed lunch menu to anyone who seemed interested—which was most people—and in between, Jia expressed her displeasure with Jennifer's newest attempt to recruit my help.

"Next she'll have you doing her grocery shopping," she remarked. "Are you sure she doesn't want you to replace Wendy?"

"I hope not." I finished sending Drew a text message with a brief summary of the morning's events. "I'd rather go into the tunnels again, thanks."

"Speaking of which, wasn't she supposed to improve the

inn's reputation among the witches in exchange for your help finding the thief?"

"She did, but now she's convinced the best way to catch the thief is to ambush them the next time they try to break into Mina's office," I said. "I guess questioning the coven members didn't come to anything—and the ones in the jail just laughed at both of us."

"They would," she said. "Still doesn't explain why she can't ask someone else."

"I'm a master of stealth." My phone buzzed in my pocket with a message from Drew saying he was on his way, no doubt with a list of more objections. "And the other Reaper isn't answering his door."

"I wonder why that is?"

"He's old Harold. He doesn't need a reason." I lifted my head to the door when I spied Drew approaching through the window. "He might be avoiding me because he knows it's his fault the thief was able to steal that book. If he'd handed it over to the Reaper Council like he was supposed to, this wouldn't have happened."

Drew entered through the doors, crossed the restaurant floor, and said, "No way."

"I knew you'd say that." I hadn't been able to share all the details of my conversation with Jennifer in a text message, but he'd gotten the gist. "It's Mart who's volunteering to hang around the coven headquarters on security duty tonight. All I'll do is jump in when he spies the intruder."

"It's the police's job to catch criminals," he said. "She didn't even file a report on last night's break-in."

"You know what she's like," I said. "She didn't report the existence of a book of illegal magic to anyone except Harold the Reaper."

"Then why help her?" His brow creased. "Altruism towards the witches isn't usually your style."

"Trust me, if it wasn't a book of necromancy we were dealing with, I'd foist this off on the first available person."

"Necromancy." Alarm flickered across his face. "That's what the book can do?"

"Only if you try using the rituals inside it." I lowered my voice to avoid freaking out the customers. "It's the sort of book the Reaper Council is supposed to confiscate, except our esteemed Reaper decided to keep it to himself and trusted the coven to keep the book safe. Needless to say, that plan backfired on both of them."

"Why doesn't *he* volunteer to catch this thief?"

"I was going to ask him, but he didn't answer the door."

"Typical." His jaw tightened in annoyance. "It's not your responsibility, Maura. No more than the tunnel is."

"You have to admit we've stalled out on finding Mina Devlin and her allies," I pointed out. "And I don't know about you, but I don't want her messing with necromancy again."

"She already summoned a demon without the need for a book," Jia reminded me. "What's to stop her from trying it again?"

"According to Jennifer, Harold implied the book could help her do worse."

"What's worse than a demon?" Jia's eyes rounded. "I thought that was the worst the afterworld had to offer?"

"There are different… levels of demons." Now we were treading too closely to the kind of secrets Reapers weren't supposed to confide in humans. Ones that'd earn me more than a slap on the wrist for sharing. "Some more powerful than others. It'd be just like Mina to try messing with monsters that would happily eat her soul, given the chance, but I'd rather not give *her* the chance to drag the rest of us down with her."

"No kidding." Jia shuddered. "You'd think Jennifer would be more inclined to try catching the thief herself, though."

"You'd think, but the thief will expect her to be watching." To Drew, I added, "Come on, I'm not going near the river this time. If you stay over in my room, you'll be a heartbeat away. Literally."

"Unless someone shuts off your Reaper powers again."

Was that what was bugging him? "If they do, I know how to remove that spell and so does Jennifer. She'll be in her own office waiting for me to spring the trap."

His mouth pressed together. "There's got to be a better way."

"Probably, but I'm all in favour of screwing up Mina Devlin's night *and* stopping her from unleashing any demonic rituals," I said. "Also, it's really weird that Wendy's been sent home. I kinda feel sorry for her."

"I don't," said Jia. "She needs to grow a backbone rather than following Jennifer everywhere. Maybe her boss got fed up with all the hand-wringing."

"That or she actually does suspect her of the theft." I didn't know, either, but there was only one good way to find out the thief's identity. "We'll find out tonight, one way or another."

Drew exhaled. "All right, but I don't think this is a good idea."

"Not my worst, though, is it?" I had an endless track record of screwups, going all the way back to my Reaper apprenticeship and even before. "If you see old Harold, tell him it's all his fault."

You'd think Harold would have told Shelton at the very least. Shelton was the one who'd taken the last book of dark magic we'd found in Hawkwood Hollow and presumably handed it over to the council, but I hadn't heard anything from him in weeks.

Except that he'd sought out my dad.

No more calls from home had interrupted my day.

Neither had any surprise visits. I wouldn't lie—I was kind of looking forward to my upcoming clash with the would-be thief, just for a little excitement.

I'll get them this time. And with a little luck, they'll lead us straight to Mina.

7

The rest of my shift flew by, with Drew coming over to the inn after he'd finished work. Mart kept everyone entertained by floating around the restaurant with the inflatable pumpkin on his head while Drew and I chatted about lighter topics, such as the Halloween event. Eventually, after the restaurant closed for the night, I convinced Mart to put away the pumpkin and go to the witches' headquarters.

While he watched out for the thief, I lay down on the bed fully clothed, prepared to be jolted out of sleep at a moment's notice when Mart returned. Drew lay beside me, equally wide-awake—though not for long. By the time midnight ticked past, Drew was sound asleep, and I was as wakeful as ever.

"Maura." Mart's voice spoke softly in my ear. "Intruder alert."

I bolted upright. "Where?"

"They just entered the building."

"Got it." I pushed off the bed and shoved my feet into my shoes. Then I stepped into the shadows in the same instant as Drew startled awake. *Sorry, Drew. I'll be back.*

I emerged out of the shadows into the darkened lobby of the witches' headquarters. Nobody was there—except for a short woman who screamed when she saw me.

"Gotcha." I jumped on top of the intruder, pinning her down with my knees. *A witch.* I didn't recognise her wildly curly dark hair or pale face, but she'd been right outside Mina's office. "Nice try."

"I—what are *you?*" she gasped. "Help!"

"I'm here to stop you from playing any more pranks on Jennifer," I informed the struggling witch. "What're you doing here, exactly?"

"Pranks?" She squinted up at me. "I came to get some supplies from the storeroom."

"In the middle of the night?"

"I thought any witch was allowed to use the storeroom at any time," she said, sounding put-out. "Unless the new leader changed the rules."

"Are you new in town?" She kept squirming underneath me, trying to push me off, but I didn't budge. "Yeah, no. I don't believe you."

"Let her go," Jennifer called from behind me. "Priscilla. I'm surprised it's you."

Reluctantly, I relaxed my hold on the witch, and she scrambled to her feet. "I—I didn't expect anyone to be here."

"I thought you left town." Jennifer stepped around me, so she stood between Priscilla and the way out. "Months ago."

"I did," said the witch. "I, ah, left for work."

"And came back a few months later?" I asked. "I don't buy it."

"The job didn't work out." Priscilla addressed Jennifer, no longer paying me any attention. "I decided to come back to somewhere familiar. I didn't know you'd hired a Reaper as your security guard."

"I'm not," I corrected. "I'm here to catch a thief. Unless

you were in the wrong place at the wrong time, which I doubt, that's you."

If Priscilla was innocent, I was a unicorn. The fact that she'd lived here when Mina Devlin had been in charge and had left after I'd ousted her leader was a screaming red flag if I ever saw one. I'd bet anything she'd gone straight to Mina after leaving and had come back to test the waters on her former coven leader's orders.

"That'll do, Maura," said Jennifer. "I'll talk to her myself."

That's it? It'd have been nice to have a thank-you at the very least, but Mart had disappeared, and I didn't want to spend any more time hanging around in the witches' headquarters than I had to. At this rate, Drew would come running over from the inn and draw even more unwanted attention.

"Fine." I turned my back on the witches and walked out.

As the doors slid closed behind me, Mart came zipping over. "Hey, Maura. There's someone hanging around the back of the headquarters."

"There is?" I peered around the corner, but the darkness between the building and its neighbour made it hard to make out any human-sized figures. "Where?"

As I moved into the darkness, movement stirred. Out of the corner of my eye, I spied a man moving at a speed that only a sharp-eyed Reaper would have no difficulty spotting. *Whoa.*

"That wasn't a ghost." Mart took off like a rocket while I backed out onto the high street where there was a little more light. Of course, the figure had long since vanished by then, but he hadn't gone into the afterworld. I'd have seen if he had.

Mart came zooming back to my side. "What's a vampire doing here?"

"You think it was a vampire?" They could certainly move

at freakishly fast speeds, though I'd never seen one in Hawkwood Hollow before. I scanned the high street, but nobody else was out this late.

"You don't believe me?" Mart sounded slightly insulted. "I know the difference between a vampire and a ghost."

"I know, but it's dark." I'd lingered out here long enough, so I called the shadows to my hands and stepped through.

I landed back in my room, where Drew jumped to his feet. "Maura. I was going to come looking for you."

"I thought you would." I kicked off my shoes. "Don't worry, we caught the intruder."

"No, we didn't," Mart countered.

I frowned at my brother. "Mart, you're the one who alerted me."

"I know, but I'm not sure that witch I caught was the thief."

"What makes you say that?" I asked. "You think it was that... whatever it was?"

"What?" Drew tracked our conversation the best he could, though he couldn't see or hear Mart. "What's up with your brother?"

"Mart thinks he saw a vampire."

"A *vampire?*"

"I *did* see a vampire," Mart corrected. "Remember a few weeks ago? I'm sure I saw him then too."

"I thought that turned out to be a ghoul."

"So did I, but it was dark, and they move fast."

"Maura, what's going on?" Drew peered at me in the darkness. "Another ghoul?"

"No, but someone was spying on the witches' headquarters," I explained. "He ran off so fast that Mart thought he was a vampire, but the witch I caught was definitely one of Mina's people, so I'm more inclined to think she was the thief than our mysterious stranger."

"I don't appreciate the disrespect!" Mart said. "Vampires are untrustworthy by nature."

"I don't disagree, but—"

"I'll send out a team." Drew reached for his phone.

"Don't bother," I said, exasperated. "Mart is in a mood, and I don't blame him, but it's not worth—"

A pillow lifted itself from the bed and threw itself at me. I backed away from the onslaught as more pillows hit me, and when I next looked up, Mart was gone.

Drew picked up a pillow and put it back on the bed. "I take it your brother isn't pleased with you?"

"He's going to flood the entire upstairs floor for this." I retrieved another pillow. "I didn't get a good look at the person spying on the witches' headquarters, and for all I know, it *was* a vampire, but… I don't know."

"Only you could run into a vampire while hunting for a thief, Maura."

"I didn't 'run into' him." I put the pillow back into place. "That's the point. Also, the witch we caught ticked all the boxes for the thief. She's a former coven member who left after Mina was ousted and then pretended that she was on a midnight supply run when I caught her."

"She's here on her former leader's orders, you think?"

"Makes more sense than a vampire being in the area." I finished putting the pillows back and sat down on the bed. "Unless they were working together."

"Why would a vampire steal from the witches?"

"Haven't a clue." And why would one work with Mina Devlin? If there *was* a vampire, he might be spying on the coven for his own reasons. Or Mart had been mistaken. Honestly, it'd be far easier if he had been.

Yeah, right. Since when was my life that simple?

———

I slept like crap for the rest of the night. Part of it was because Mart kept coming into the room and making loud noises intended to wake me up, but my own thoughts did a decent job of keeping me awake regardless. I kept thinking I saw shadowy figures in the corners, too, but it was more likely to be my obnoxious brother than a vampire.

Eventually, I dragged my sorry self out of bed to grab breakfast from the lobby, and when Drew left for work, I decided to drop in and see what Jennifer had done with the thief after I'd gone back to my room.

If Priscilla had indeed been the one to steal the book, Jennifer ought to have got it back by now, which meant I didn't have to do any more for the coven. If not… Well, I needed to know either way.

Like the previous day, Wendy wasn't there to greet me at the doors, and I walked up to Jennifer's office without being accosted. I half expected to find Priscilla in there, like the time I'd found Mart imprisoned in a circle of sage, but instead Jennifer sat alone behind her desk.

"Did you let Priscilla go?" I asked her. "Or hand her over to the police?"

"The latter, after I finished questioning her," she replied.

An interesting choice on her part. "Did she admit to breaking in and stealing the book?"

"No, but I decided that a few days in the holding cells might loosen her tongue."

"She didn't have the book with her?" Suspicion prickled between my shoulder blades. "My brother thinks he saw a vampire outside at the same time he caught the thief."

"A vampire?" She raised a brow. "Your brother the ghost, you mean?"

"I don't have any other brothers, so yes," I said. "I'm not sure I believe he did see one, but I figured you might want to know."

"What makes him think it was a vampire?" she queried.

"The guy moved really fast."

"Not a Reaper?"

"No, I can sense Reapers." I hadn't thought to check the afterworld, come to think of it, but vampires were also untraceable through the afterworld. One of many reasons they didn't get along with Reapers. "Would Mina have hired one, do you think?"

"It wouldn't be out of character for her," she said. "I'll keep an eye out, but I suspect Priscilla was indeed the thief. I've every intention of searching her house later, though that would be too obvious a hiding place."

"She has a house, then?" I asked. "I thought she left town."

"She did but not permanently. Her story added up, for what it's worth."

If she's not the thief, why'd she come back? "You still handed her over to the police?"

"Yes," she replied. "The officer I spoke to implied that the theft wasn't worth investigating as a serious crime, but she reluctantly agreed to keep Priscilla in the holding cells on suspicion of breaking and entering."

"Was that Petra, by any chance?"

"Yes, it was." She rose to her feet. "I believe I'll search Priscilla's house now. Do you want to come with me?"

"I have to get to work." After my sleepless night, I was hardly in the mood for drama, and I had every intention of keeping my head down and not stirring up trouble.

When I made a comment to this effect to Jia as we were starting work, Mart laughed loudly enough to rattle all the nearby glasses on the bar. "That'll be the day."

"Oi." I faced Jia, who grinned. "What?"

"He has a point," she said. "You apprehended a thief *and* ran into a vampire before sunrise. I dread to think what other shenanigans you'll get up to today."

"Vampire," I repeated. "You believe Mart, then?"

Mart upended a glass of water on my head. I gaped, too startled to retaliate at first, and then lunged at him with a motion that only caused my sopping wet hair to smack me in the face. Spitting out curses, I pulled out my wand. Jia was doubled over with laughter.

"Thanks a lot." I waved my wand to dry my hair. "If I was the one who claimed I saw a vampire in the dark, you'd think I was losing my mind too."

"I'm a ghost," Mart said. "I lost my last marble a long time ago."

"Precisely." I raised my wand in warning in case he tried tipping water onto my head again. "I'm not saying you aren't telling the truth, but if the vampire's the thief, why come back to the coven headquarters and draw attention to himself?"

"You said Jennifer handed the culprit over to the police?" Jia asked me. "What was her name again?"

"Priscilla Leyton."

She gave a low whistle. "I know her."

"You've met?"

"Yeah, but…" She paused. "But she wasn't close to Mina when she lived here. Seems odd."

"Not really," I said. "Mina's biggest supporters are in jail. She must be running out of people to send to taunt me."

"She's also powerful enough to coerce others into obeying her," she said. "Vampires, though… I have to admit, I can understand why they might get along. The older vampires are as ruthless as she is."

"They're also loners who look out for their own."

"Maybe they made a deal." Jia shrugged. "I don't know. Or the vampire came here looking for employment."

"At the inn?" I snorted. "Actually, a vampire might not be

the worst person to have on staff. If nothing else, evening shifts would be easy to outsource."

Jia grinned. "Yeah, even vampires have to pay bills."

Most vampires were old enough to have amassed a small fortune, of course, but the vampire conversation kept us entertained all morning without causing us to bring up subjects that were considerably less pleasant. Our debate over whether a vampire would agree to participate in our ghost tours caused even Mart's mood to improve, though he drew the line at being upstaged.

"Relax—no vampire would agree to work in the same building as a Reaper," I told him.

"Why's that?" asked Jia. "You don't get along. Is it like the infamous vampire and werewolf rivalry?"

"Kind of," I replied. "I think the Reaper Council dislikes vampires because they're undying, and their souls don't go anywhere after they wake from death. They make a huge deal about it being unnatural, which is rich, coming from the Reapers."

"Did they—?" Jia's mouth slammed shut when the door opened, and Petra strode into the restaurant, eyeing the Halloween decorations with her usual expression of disdain. "Hi, Petra. Can I help you?"

"I saw you sneaking around town last night," she said to me, ignoring Jia altogether. "After dark."

"Is that illegal now?" What was her problem this time?

"Am I supposed to believe you were idling around the high street for innocent reasons?" she enquired.

"I went to do the witches a favour. Nothing dodgy about that." Jennifer hadn't sent her after me, surely, had she? "Didn't you apprehend the thief I helped the coven leader catch in their headquarters?"

"You need to stop trying to do the police's jobs," she spat out. "I've given you more than enough warnings."

"Jennifer asked me to help," I told her. "And you're welcome."

"Your attitude needs adjusting, Reaper."

Speak for yourself. Luckily, Allie entered the restaurant before I could reply and dig myself a deeper hole. Eyeing Petra, she asked, "Is there a problem?"

"One of your employees has been walking around the town at night."

"I don't monitor what my employees do in their spare time," she said. "And Maura hasn't broken any laws."

"That remains to be seen."

"What's that supposed to mean?" I asked. Had someone been spreading stories about me? "The criminal is the person who broke into the witches' headquarters, not me."

"An interesting way of putting it," she said. "I thought you claimed to have caught the thief."

"I did." If she was trying to put together an excuse to lock *me* up as well, she was barking up the wrong tree. "Jennifer asked me to catch the next person who broke into the headquarters. I did, and she handed them to you. Nothing more."

"So you weren't running around the police station at night?"

"I wasn't, no." *Wait.* "Someone broke in there as well?"

"Yes, they did." Her nostrils flared. "Not long before I spied *you* wandering around the high street."

Never mind the thief—what was Petra *doing out last night?* "Was it Priscilla?"

"No," she said. "It wasn't a witch but someone who moved far quicker than a human."

A Reaper? Or a vampire? "Didn't anyone else see them?"

"I'll certainly be making enquiries." She cast a glare around the room.

Allie crossed the room to address her in a firm tone.

"Maura didn't break into the police station. She was right here—with Drew."

Petra's eyes narrowed. "The head of the police needs to be careful not to let his romantic entanglements cloud his judgement."

"Sure, I broke into the police station while the head officer was asleep in my room." I gave her an eye-roll. "I might remind you that I'm not the only Reaper around here. Ask Harold." If nothing else, it might convince him to show his face for once.

Petra surveyed the restaurant with an expression that suggested she wished she'd brought more of the Wardens' ogres to arrest me again, and then she turned her back and walked away.

As the doors slid closed behind her, I turned to Jia in bewilderment. "What was that about?"

"No clue," said Jia. "She can't really think you broke into the police station, can she?"

"It was the vampire!" Mart announced. "I knew it. Now do you believe me?"

"If it was the vampire—"

"What vampire?" Allie interjected.

"Mart thinks he saw one last night—and he might have," I added when he waved a glass of water threateningly at me again. "A vampire fits the description of what Petra saw— someone who moved too quickly for her to see his face."

"You can sense other Reapers, can't you?" Jia asked.

"I can, and I didn't sense one last night," I said. "If Petra decides to call the Wardens again, she'll be doing me a favour."

"Again?" Allie's jaw dropped. "She was the one who called them?"

"She never directly admitted to it, but it's obvious." I lowered my voice, conscious that the few customers in the restaurant had noticed the altercation. "Luckily, I have Perry's team on my side in case it happens again, but it's weird that someone broke into the police station as well as the witches' headquarters. I hope they weren't visiting Mina's allies in jail."

I pulled out my phone to text Drew, though he should already know about the break-in if Petra had told him, which she ought to have done. I was willing to bet she hadn't mentioned that she intended to come here and interrogate me, though.

"What *were* you doing last night, anyway, Maura?" asked Allie.

"Helping Jennifer Ness catch a thief," I said. "Whom she handed over to the police without so much as a thank-you. That's the last time I do her a favour."

"She has to hold up her end of the bargain now, though," Jia said as we returned to work, with considerably less cheer than before. "Which means investigating the tunnels and telling her witches to stop avoiding the inn like the plague."

"Unless it turns out Priscilla wasn't the thief." Priscilla hadn't broken into the police station, had she? "She panicked and fought back when I caught her, but that's what tends to happen when a Reaper jumps out of the afterworld and lands on top of you. Maybe I made the wrong call."

"You could always talk to our friendly neighbourhood Reaper," Jia suggested. "I bet he'll know if there's a vampire in town."

"Vampires don't usually haunt graveyards."

"Unless they're in the market for coffins to sleep in," added Mart. "He *might* have seen our fanged intruder and forgot to mention it, like he did with the book of doom."

"Maybe." Harold would have noticed if a vampire had taken up permanent residence here, even though they only came out at dusk. Vampires didn't turn to dust in daylight—

or sparkle, come to that—but they were generally night creatures that slept during daylight hours.

The other issue with vampires was that they moved fast enough to traverse half the country in a day if they were so inclined. Granted, they didn't tend to exert themselves unless they had good reason, and it felt like this one was local.

Regardless, Harold and I were long overdue a conversation and not just about the book and the vampire. Was he the one who'd sent Shelton to talk to my family? I hadn't heard from my hometown since that initial call, but the thought remained in the back of my mind.

Next time I visited the Reaper, I'd make sure he answered me.

8

I had to wait until after the lunchtime rush before I had a spare hour to pay the Reaper a visit. When I crossed the bridge outside the inn, I had a quick peek underneath, but the lower water levels hadn't quite cleared the tunnel entrance yet.

"That's a good hiding place for a vampire, that is," Mart remarked.

"They hate water." Admittedly, the vampire on the Wardens' team had jumped into the river to save Perry and me from a watery grave, but that incident was an exception rather than a rule.

"Maybe this one has a death wish," Mart said. "An undeath wish, I mean. He already broke into the police station for a prank."

"If that was a vampire, it was no prank," I murmured, thinking of the absolute smugness of Mina's allies when I'd visited the jail. "Let's see if our Reaper has seen him."

When we reached the local graveyard, I knocked on the Reaper's door and got the customary "go away" reaction, which was better than silence.

"Good, you're in this time," I called back. "I want a word with you."

"Then say it."

"She didn't mean only *one* word," Mart interjected. "I have one for you, though it's not meant for polite company."

"What?" The door flew open, and old Harold appeared in the entryway. "Haven't you caught your thief yet?"

"You didn't tell me Mina had books of illegal necromancy hidden in her cabinet," I accused him. "Nor did you mention it to any other Reapers."

"I thought you didn't want the council snooping around here." He rested a hand on the door frame, revealing the scythe that stood behind him. The curved instrument might have been more intimidating if he wasn't using it as a coatrack. "Blame the witches, not me."

"Oh no, you aren't getting off the hook." I jammed my foot against the doorframe to prevent him from shutting the door in my face. "What exactly were you thinking? Even without telling the council, you might have told *me* there were illegal books of necromancy in the witches' head-quarters."

"And you'd have done what you normally do," he said, "and drawn unwanted attention."

Mart laughed in my ear. "He has a point there."

"Don't you take *his* side." I scowled at the Reaper. "Also, was it you who sent Shelton to talk to my family?"

That got his attention. "Family?"

"My dad"—I slipped through the door before he could shut me out and planted myself in the hallway—"Shelton went to see him and let slip my new address, so I wondered if you heard from our Reaper friend recently."

"Define 'recent.'"

"That means you *have* heard from him," I surmised. "Why in hell didn't you give Shelton the book, then? He could have handed it to the council without mentioning where he got it."

"I had no desire to start a feud with the new coven leader. She was quite adamant that she wanted the book to stay in her predecessor's office."

"And now its previous owner has stolen it back." I rolled my eyes at him. "Well done."

"Did you just come here to reprimand me?" he asked. "Because if I were to list *your* mistakes, we'd be here all day."

"I came here to find out what you were thinking when you let Mina get hold of a book that would let her do worse than she did with the floods. That was what you told Jennifer, wasn't it?"

Shadows surged around his feet, and for an instant, I wondered if he was about to pick up the scythe after all— then his shoulders slumped. "It was Jennifer Ness's mistake, not mine. She was the one who was lax with her security."

"She wasn't," I said. "The thief got through a locked door that only two people could access. More than once, if it's the same person who keeps breaking in on a nightly basis."

"Precisely," he said. "Her mistake. Not mine."

"You're allergic to the concept of responsibility, aren't you?" I could see why he'd believe the witches had sealed their own fate when they'd decided to keep hold of a book that should never have been in their possession. Still, someone had to deal with the situation. "And before you ask why it matters to me, I volunteered to catch the thief in exchange for access to a certain tunnel, among other things."

"What?" The shadows disappeared as he stared at me in alarm. "Do you *want* to drown this time?"

"Obviously not." Hadn't he wanted me to find proof of Mina Devlin's misdeeds? "I never said I'd go in there myself, but certain police officers won't believe anything they don't experience with their own senses."

"I thought that werewolf partner of yours was head of the police."

"He is." As well Harold knew. "But Drew didn't come into the tunnel with me, and I didn't exactly have the chance to get photographic evidence when I was nearly drowning."

"You won't need it if Mina truly does have that book," he said. "I'd advise you to keep your attention there, not on the past."

"I already caught the thief." Wasn't he the one who'd told me the truth of the town's history in the first place? Under duress, admittedly, but still. "Jennifer is going to find out where she stashed the book and retrieve it."

"There you have it, then." He indicated the door. "Go and help her."

Mart flew in front of me. "Now I'm going to hang around and annoy you all day. Also, have you seen any vampires?"

"Have you a sudden desire to see the wrong end of my scythe?" Harold retaliated.

"*Have* you seen any vampires?" I peered around my brother. "Mart thinks he saw one the other night, so I figured you might have."

"I *did* see one, and so did that idiot police officer," Mart interjected.

"No, I certainly haven't seen any vampires." Harold waved an impatient hand. "Get out, both of you."

"C'mon." I beckoned to my brother, giving up on the crochety old Reaper. "We're wasting our time here."

Harold hadn't seen the vampire, and he'd fall on his own scythe before he admitted any culpability in the book's theft. I was kind of tempted to drop by the police station on the way back to ask if any other officers had seen the supposed break-in, but that would land me in trouble with Petra yet again. No, I'd ask Drew later instead.

When we reached the high street, Mart veered and drifted away from me.

"Mart, where are you going?" I called after him.

He didn't answer, so I followed his path as he moved towards the blocky building on the corner that housed the local hospital. "Mart—what are you doing?"

"Vampires," he said, inexplicably, and floated straight through the doors and into the reception area.

Okay, he's lost it. I stood awkwardly in the doorway for a long moment before the obvious occurred to me. If anyone would know if there was a vampire in town—assuming said vampire wasn't attacking locals and biting them instead of using the local blood bank—it was the hospital staff.

Not to mention that a certain ex-ally of Mina Devlin worked there.

I stepped into the hospital and made for the corridor off the lobby, where I knocked on the door to the one room I'd visited before.

"What?" called a familiar irritable voice.

I pushed open the door, revealing a grumpy witch with frizzy hair seated behind a cauldron. It was Cathy, the coven healer, who rolled her eyes when she saw me.

"Not you again," she grouched. "Let me guess. Jennifer sent you."

"Nope, she hasn't a clue I'm here." I stepped into the room and closed the door behind me. "Also, I'm not here for the reason you think."

"What, you aren't here to accuse me of petty breaking and entering?" she said. "Good, because I've already had to give Jennifer my weekly shift schedule to prove I was at work at night when the break-in happened. There are witnesses."

"It's a different kind of break-in I'm here to ask about." I was probably speaking to the wrong person, but Cathy was a known connection to Mina Devlin. "Has the blood bank acquired any new visitors lately? Of the fanged variety?"

She scoffed. "Funny you should say that. We have had a few weird incidents with samples going missing."

"Blood samples?"

"Yes, but if there's a vampire swiping them, it's better than biting the locals."

"True, I guess." *Someone is stealing from the blood bank?* "Would Mina Devlin work with one, do you think?"

"With a vampire? She'd work with anyone who stroked her ego." She lowered her gaze to the bubbling cauldron. "And yes, I know something was stolen from the old coven leader's office, but I have no idea what. Talk to Jennifer, not me."

"I already did," I said. "Also… did *you* know about the tunnels?"

"No." Cathy gave the contents of the cauldron a stir. "I don't really care if you believe me or otherwise, but I was never close enough to Mina to be entrusted with confidential information. Whatever she was doing down in those tunnels, I have no idea. I'm a healer, not a practitioner of dark magic."

Dark magic. "That was what you think she was doing?"

"If she wasn't, she'd have been out in the open, not skulking underground."

True enough, and maybe I was wrong to be suspicious of her. But that didn't change the fact that Mart had been right.

There *was* a vampire in town.

———

My brother was as insufferable as I'd expected when I told him about the missing blood samples. He gloated all the way back to the inn about how he'd been right all along and that I owed him a profound apology.

"All right," I relented, entering the restaurant. "I'm sorry for doubting you. Now, will you talk about literally anything else for the rest of our shift?"

"That wasn't part of the bargain." He flew across the room, whooping, while a baffled Jia watched from the counter.

"What in the world happened?" she asked. "Did your brother win the ghostly lottery or something?"

"Nope, he found proof there's a vampire hanging around town," I explained. "Stealing blood samples from the hospital."

"Better than stealing humans to nibble on." Jia watched Mart perform loop-the-loops in midair. "Is the vampire the one who stole from the witches, too, though?"

"I expect we'll find out if Jennifer managed to find anything in Priscilla's house soon," I said. "If I can be bothered to drag myself up there again today."

"At least the Reaper answered the door this time."

"Not that he was much help." Mart might be in a great mood, but a metaphorical thundercloud hung over my head, not at all helped by my knowledge that if the vampire *was* the thief, we didn't have a clue where he was hiding.

"I told you, the vampire's in the tunnel," Mart said when I mentioned this aloud.

"Really?" Jia shrugged. "I guess it's dark enough in there. No noisy humans intruding."

"Mart, you didn't see him hiding in the tunnel the last time you went in there, did you?" I pointed out. "The police are going to come to a decision soon about whether to send in a team, so I guess we'll find out soon enough."

"No, they aren't," he said. "That Petra will probably keep them arguing for months."

"Not if she thinks there might be a connection with whoever broke into the police station."

"That was the vampire too?" Jia blinked at me. "Why break in there? Oh, right. Mina's allies?"

"You've got it." Maybe that accounted for my sense of unease, though I couldn't stifle the worry that the witches *wouldn't* find the missing book in the house of the supposed thief. If the vampire had it instead, was there a better hiding place than Mina's former lair?

When Carey entered the restaurant, having come back from school, my phone buzzed with a message from Drew. *The officers have agreed to send a team into the tunnels tomorrow.*

"What?" I yelped, nearly dropping my phone. "He's sending in a team?"

"To the tunnels?" Jia peered over my shoulder. "I guess Jennifer kept her word. And he got Petra to cave after all."

"I guess she's more interested in finding the source of the break-in than arguing for the sake of it."

"If she was the only witness, I bet nobody else gives a crap." Mart snickered to himself. "I hope she gets lost in the dark. It'd be hilarious."

Carey came scurrying over to Jia and me, putting down her schoolbag. "What break-in?"

"Someone broke into the police station last night," I said evasively. "Petra blamed me, because she has a screw loose."

"Weren't you out last night?"

"For about ten minutes." I'd told Carey that I'd helped catch a thief before she left for school that morning, but I hadn't given her any details. I didn't need to cause her pointless worry by mentioning tomes of dark magic and sinister figures lurking in the darkness. "I didn't go near the police station, though, so I have no idea what she was thinking."

"Petra will want to be on the team that gets into the tunnels," Jia remarked. "She won't stand for sitting that one out."

"She also doesn't want to dirty her hands." I was starting

to wish I'd pushed to be allowed on the team myself. "I don't know that they'll be able to find much in there. If the kind of magic the coven was doing in there is visible only to Reapers…"

"Not again, Maura." Jia tutted. "Nearly drowning wasn't enough for you? You want to go back in?"

"I know what to expect this time. I also know how to use a water-breathing spell."

"And if there's a murderous coven down there?"

"There won't be."

A vampire, though? That was a possibility, and the police certainly wouldn't be prepared to deal with one.

Carey had gone pale. "You aren't going into the tunnel, are you?"

"Someone is," I said. "It doesn't have to be me, but the police are sending a team to look around, and I've been in there before."

"So have I," Mart said.

"You can come too," I told my brother. "I'll ask Drew. He won't be able to deny it'll be quicker with a guide."

"Why?" Carey burst out. "Why do you need to risk your life?"

"For proof." I waved my new phone in the air—a replacement for the one that'd gotten an unfortunate soaking. "Last time, I got taken by surprise. It won't happen again."

Drew, of course, saw things differently. When he showed up later that evening and I announced my plan, he went through a long list of the usual arguments, which I rebutted one at a time. I finished up by saying that unless I landed directly on top of a demon, I was unlikely to end up in any danger.

"Maura, if anyone could land directly on top of a demon, it's you," was his response.

"Hmm." Maybe I shouldn't have used that particular

example. "If we make sure to remove any magical defences Mina might have put on the tunnels, it won't be any riskier than your officers going in."

"My people are paid to take risks," he said. "I don't like the idea of them going in there, either, but they volunteered."

"So did I," I said. "Also, Mart will be with me, and I'll take all the precautions I can."

"That won't guarantee anything." His mouth turned down at the corners. "I only announced the plan to dissuade Petra from making more absurd accusations."

"What?" *Not her again.* "Is she still going on about the break-in at the police station?"

"Yes, and she's certain *you* were involved."

I choked on a laugh. "Yeah, right."

"It was the vampire," Mart announced. "He broke into the police station, the hospital, *and* the coven headquarters. He's been busy."

The vampire. Even if he wasn't in the tunnel, the team deserved to know what they were getting into.

"I told her to stop being ridiculous," Drew said. "In the end, I sent her and some others to check on the tunnels earlier this afternoon. The water levels have lowered enough that it's safe to go in through the entrance outside Hawkwood Hollow."

"I wondered about that," I said. "If Mina's people start using the tunnel again, that's the entrance they'll use."

"Yes, I expect so," he said. "I'll have to decide what to do about that, as the tunnel entrance isn't inside Hawkwood Hollow itself, strictly speaking. That entrance is not my team's responsibility to supervise, but the tunnels themselves very much are."

"Yes." Then, prompted by my brother's nudging, I added, "Mart thinks there's a vampire in there."

"A vampire?" His brows rose. "In the tunnel? Not the one who was with the Wardens?"

"No, the one Mart thinks broke into the coven headquarters," I clarified. "Possibly, it was the same vampire who broke into the police station. Vampires move fast enough that they can be mistaken for Reapers, and someone's been stealing from the local blood bank too."

Drew blinked. "This is the first I've heard of it."

"The hospital staff might not have thought it was worth reporting missing blood samples to the police," I guessed. "Even Jennifer wouldn't necessarily believe there was a vampire sneaking around headquarters. She thinks she already caught the thief."

"The last time we spoke, she had yet to find the missing book," Drew said.

"Exactly," I said. "Priscilla might have just been in the wrong place at the wrong time and never had the book at all."

"I thought it was Mina you wanted to catch out," he said. "Isn't that why you wanted to go into the tunnels again? To find proof of her crimes?"

"Yes, but I figured your team should know there might be a vampire in there," I said. "I know they're difficult to fight. Even for a shifter."

"If I suggested there was a vampire hiding in there, I'd get laughed out of the room," he said. "I'll tell them to be prepared for hostility, but there's a limit."

"All the more reason for me to come with you." I pushed my argument until he grudgingly agreed to ask his officers to let me accompany the team. I expected I'd face more resistance when I showed up the following morning, but I was officially in.

If there's really a vampire hiding in there, I'll catch him myself.

9

The following morning, I set off from the inn to meet with the team of police officers Drew had selected to search the tunnels. I followed the path of the river eastward while Mart drifted behind me, humming under his breath. I did my best to ignore the twinge of guilt in my chest at how I'd intentionally left the inn before Carey had come downstairs and before Jia had shown up for work to avoid unnecessary questions.

I also hadn't mentioned the vampire to the other officers. That might come back to bite me—pun intended—but I wasn't sure my brother was right about the vampire making his home down in the tunnels.

When we reached the outskirts of Hawkwood Hollow, Mart and I crossed another bridge to the area I recognised as where I'd emerged from my near drowning. The tunnel entrance was farther from the town itself than I'd realised, nestled beneath the bridge and surrounded by gathering police officers.

Drew waylaid me first. "Maura, are you sure about this?"

"Absolutely." Dropping my voice, I added, "If there's

anything inside the tunnels that's visible only to a Reaper, your team should be glad to have my brother and me in there."

"Your brother is coming too?"

"Yes, he is." Leaving him behind was out of the question. "Is the entrance clear? No booby traps?"

"I'll send a couple of people ahead. Both volunteers are wizards, so they'll be able to remove any hostile security spells."

"I hope you're right." I watched Mart float over to the tunnel entrance ahead of the two wary-looking officers Drew had selected. I didn't know either of them well, but since they were wizards, they did at least have some ability to handle Mina's sneaky security spells.

A vampire, though? I had my doubts.

I trod closer to the tunnel entrance as the two wizards disappeared inside. "Drew, I think I should lead the way."

"Maura." He lowered his voice. "I have to let my team maintain some level of control here."

"If there's a trap in there, it's meant for me." I was also prepared this time. "Can I just—"

"Watch out!" The cry came from within the tunnel entrance, and one of the wizards came bolting out of there as if a manticore were on his tail. Behind him, his fellow officer screamed from somewhere in the dark.

Drew swore and moved closer, but in order to properly see into the tunnel, he'd have to go inside.

"I'm going in," I told him, pulling out my wand and casting a light spell. "Ready?"

Drew inclined his head and descended the bank while I used my wand to illuminate the tunnel entrance. Inside, the second officer lay groaning on the floor, but there was no sign of his attacker.

"Who was it?" Drew asked.

The officer winced, pressed his hands to his neck, and his fingers came away red. "A… I think it was a vampire."

"Crap." My body tensed. "He *is* hiding in here."

"I knew it!" Mart yelled in triumph. "Take that, doubters."

"Mart," I said out of the corner of my mouth, "please do everyone a favour and chase down the vampire instead of gloating."

"Who're you talking to?" The officer pushed himself upright, looking wildly around the tunnel.

"Never mind." I'd had enough of screwing around. "Drew —sorry about this—I'm going after our interloper."

I took off at a run, sprinting ahead into the darkness, while Drew's shout echoed off the walls behind me. *Sorry, Drew, but only a Reaper stands a chance of catching a vampire.*

A Reaper—or a ghost. My brother had the lead, but the vampire had gone when I caught up to Mart.

"You know even you can't outrun a vampire, don't you?" he said.

"Wasn't my plan." I called the afterworld and leapt into the shadows. As I did so, I pictured the first chamber Perry and I had come to when we'd walked in here the first time.

The shadows receded, and I ran out of the dark into the stone-walled chamber, shining my wand's light ahead of me. The vampire wasn't here, but the pattern of glyphs on the walls seemed brighter than before. I recognised some of them, but Jennifer Ness would surely know the others.

All right. Keeping hold of my wand in one hand, I pulled out my phone with the other and snapped pictures of the glyphs. When I was done, I pocketed my phone and shone my wand's light across the entrance of the tunnel branching off the chamber. The vampire must be somewhere in there.

"Hey!" Mart came zipping into view. "You left me behind."

"Sorry." I shone my wand over the walls. "Where's our vampire?"

"Behind you!"

A heavy form crashed into me, sending both of us flying. I landed on my back, the vampire's pale face looming above me. White teeth gleamed, sharp and bared, while I fought to push him off. "What are you doing in here, Reaper?"

"Lying in the wet and cold." Dammit, I'd dropped my wand somewhere when he'd crashed into me. "What are *you* doing in here? I didn't know vampires liked damp tunnels so much."

"None of your concern, Reaper."

"You made it my concern when you landed on me." I could theoretically escape through the afterworld, but that would risk losing him when I dearly wanted to know what he was doing in the tunnel—and how long he'd been in town. "You broke into the witches' headquarters, didn't you? And the police station. Why?"

In answer, he tried to bite me. I squirmed away from his teeth and struck out, but my fist connected with his neck instead of his face.

"Stop struggling, Reaper," he growled. "It'll be easier for you."

"I beg to differ." Dammit. I'd forgotten how *strong* vampires were. His arms were like solid metal weighing me down, and those fangs were too close to my neck for my liking. "What did you do with the book? You *are* the thief, aren't you?"

"You need to learn not to poke your nose where it doesn't belong." His eyes glittered with malice. "I wonder, can a Reaper survive their throat being torn out?"

As his teeth came down, I rolled to the side. His grip didn't break, but at least his teeth sank into my arm and not my neck. *Ow.*

"Hey!" I shook my arm, pain shooting up to my shoulder. "Get your fangs out of me. I have allies waiting on both ends of this tunnel, you know. If you kill me down here, they'll come and find you."

"They'll never find me." His voice was muffled, his teeth wedged in my arm. Then he withdrew and went for my neck again.

Screw this. I called the shadows and pulled the vampire with me into the afterworld.

Darkness surrounded us in a flat, black haze. The vampire stopped mid-lunge, eyes widening when he realised where I'd taken him. As his grip slackened, I broke free and seized his wrists in mine.

Since I had the upper hand, I pictured the riverbank, and we emerged from the darkness—straight on top of Drew.

"Ah!" I let go of the vampire with one hand when he rolled off Drew then grabbed my adversary's arm again before he could make a break for it. "Drew—a little help here?"

Drew evidently hadn't expected me to land on top of him holding a rogue vampire, and from the growl that ripped from his throat, I half expected him to shift into his werewolf form. He recovered in time to stop himself, staring at both of us. "Maura—?"

"Help me hold this guy." I tightened my grip on the struggling vampire's arms. "We can't let him escape."

Drew seized him from behind, grunting in surprise when the vampire gave a wild lunge and dragged both of them forward, breaking my grip on his arms in the process.

"Don't blink." Jia popped up and pointed her wand at the vampire, and he collapsed into a heap at Drew's feet. "Sorry, Maura. I couldn't let you come here alone."

I surveyed the vampire, my injured arm throbbing. "I'm not alone."

Not that Drew's officers were doing much except gawping at the whole spectacle. Drew, for his part, began handcuffing the vampire. "Maura, what did I say about not running off alone?"

"Hey, at least I didn't land on top of a demon instead of a vampire." I held up my throbbing arm. "Might need to get this looked at, though."

"Yes, you do." He jerked his head at the other officers. "Some help would be appreciated."

"Is anyone else still in the tunnel?" I queried. "Because… ah. I left my wand behind."

I'd also left my brother, come to that.

"You're not going back in," Drew said flatly. "Not before you get that arm seen to."

"I'll get your wand," Jia offered. "I—oh, I stand corrected."

As I turned my head, a wand came flying through the air and hit me in the forehead. *Ow.* I spun around in search of the culprit and saw Mart gesturing at the wand that had rolled to a stop at my feet, its end still glowing with the light spell I'd cast. "You're welcome."

"Sorry I left you behind." I picked up my wand and extinguished the spell. "At least we caught your vampire."

The vampire chose that moment to jerk awake, and upon realising he was in handcuffs, he spewed a stream of curses that caused most of the officers to back away from him. Drew, the exception, grabbed the vampire's cuffed hands and gave him a warning shake. Undeterred, the vampire hissed and spat and generally acted like a feral cat.

"Charming, isn't he?" I stepped up to Drew, careful not to go within range of those sharp teeth. "Might want to get him a muzzle."

The other officers didn't want to get too close to his fangs, either, so Drew ended up shoving the vampire in front of him as we walked back towards Hawkwood Hollow.

Jia fell into step with me. "You aren't going to turn into a vampire, are you?"

"Nope," I replied. "It's not possible for Reapers. We're pretty much polar opposites, in magical terms."

"I thought that was vampires and shifters."

"Them too." My bleeding arm was really starting to hurt by now. "Mart—what are you doing?"

My brother had flown behind the vampire and started to blow on the back of his head, which did not improve the prisoner's mood. He bared his teeth and hissed and tried to swipe at the air—which suggested he could see exactly who, and what, was tailing him. *He can see ghosts, can he?*

"Stop it," I told my brother. "You don't need to make Drew's life difficult."

"Your brother?" Drew guessed, having long since grown used to seeing me have conversations with thin air.

"Yep." When the vampire twisted around to glare at me, I gave him an equally stony look in response. "He's got a personal grudge against our fanged friend. Now I do too."

"The vampire can see ghosts?" Jia murmured as we walked down one of the streets on the outskirts of town.

"Apparently so." I wanted to talk to the guy myself but preferably while he was behind bars and unable to bite anyone. "Must've been a wizard while he was alive."

Not uncommon, since shifters couldn't be turned into vampires, like most other paranormals. Witches and wizards, on the other hand...

When we neared the high street, Drew handed the vampire off to two of his other officers and addressed Jia. "I can trust you to take Maura to the hospital while I deal with this, can't I?"

"That's unnecessary," I objected. "I heal fast. Besides, I want to talk to the prisoner."

"Maura." Drew eyed my arm. "Can Reapers turn into vampires?"

"Nope, and even if they could, I'd need to drink *his* blood to complete the transformation," I said. "Which isn't happening in a million years. It's more important that I hear what he has to say."

"About that stolen book?" Jia guessed. "You didn't find it in the tunnels?"

"Didn't have time to explore all of them before that guy jumped me," I replied. "All right, Drew, fine. If I go to the hospital, will you let me talk to the vampire later?"

He worked his jaw. "Deal."

When we turned into the high street, however, there were several officers waiting outside the police station, including my least favourite. To no surprise, Petra instantly zeroed in on me—and on the vampire. "Who's this?"

"We caught him trespassing in the tunnels," Drew told her. "It seems he's been taunting the witches as well."

"And I bet he was the one who broke into the police station the other day," I added. "An apology would be nice."

Petra's face reddened. "You're bleeding."

"Vampires tend to be bitey."

"C'mon." Jia took my uninjured arm. "Let's get that looked at."

Resigned, I let her lead me away towards the hospital, as over his shoulder, the vampire shot me a scathing look that immediately turned into a smirk.

"What's that mean?" I took a step forward, but the officers dragged him into the police station and out of sight.

"Huh?" Jia asked. "What's wrong?"

"The vampire looked weirdly *happy*." A chill raced down my spine. "Did he get himself caught on purpose?"

―――――

"There really was a vampire?" Jennifer Ness stared at me from behind her desk. "I did wonder... but Priscilla seemed to be the obvious thief."

"I know." I held up my bloody sleeve in demonstration. I'd let Jia drag me to the hospital so that they could patch me up, then I reluctantly went to the witches' headquarters to inform Jennifer that we'd caught her intruder. "The police said he was called Jacob Reed."

"I know that name." Her brow furrowed. "I'm sure he lived here once… as a human."

"Figures." My arm gave another throb. The staff at the hospital had fixed me up in a second, but I still had a nice set of teeth-shaped marks on my arm that would take a while to fade. Jia had wanted me to go back to the inn, but I'd insisted she go ahead to tell Allie I was okay. I'd had to promise not to get into any more scuffles with any vampires, but I was working under the assumption that Jacob Reed had been alone in there.

I hope he was. And just what had that smirk been about?

"That would explain why we didn't find the book in Priscilla's house," Jennifer said. "We searched thoroughly."

"It might be in the tunnels," I admitted, "but I didn't have time to look around everywhere before the vampire jumped on me."

"Did he mention my predecessor's name?"

"He didn't mention anything at all," I said. "He told me to mind my own business, and… Honestly, he seemed almost grateful that I caught him. Unless I was reading him wrong."

"Why would that be the case?"

"That's what I'd like to know too." It left me ill at ease, though I certainly felt more secure with the vampire behind bars than running around unchecked. "I did get some photos of the spells Mina used in the tunnels. Want to see them?"

"Of course." She watched as I fished my phone out of my pocket. "This is the evidence we need to prove Mina was dabbling in illegal magic."

"I didn't recognise all the symbols." I pulled up the images of the tunnel walls, lit by wand-light, and passed her my phone. "This was the main chamber."

"I see." She pointed her wand at the phone, performing a spell that would transfer the photos to her computer. "I'll certainly examine these closely. At a glance, it looks like ritual magic… and spells to prevent intruders from entering."

When she handed me my phone back, I cleared my throat. "Ah—are you going to let Priscilla go? Is she still in jail?"

"I'll talk to the police later," she said. "There's a chance she and the vampire were working together."

Hmm. I had my doubts, but I wanted to talk to the vampire myself regardless. "We still need to find where he hid the book, but I don't know that he'll give it away easily."

"If it's in the tunnels, I intend to send some of my own people to search."

I was less than certain the police would let her, but they might be too distracted by the vampire to pay attention to the coven leader, and she'd managed to convince them to let her enter the jail once already. I'd rather they keep their attention on their fanged prisoner, as I didn't trust the guy to stay contained in a cell. Vampires were notoriously good at slipping through the cracks, and his reaction to the arrest had made me suspicious to say the least.

I walked to the police station and was greeted by a stern-faced Petra. "No."

"What do you mean, 'no'?"

"You aren't coming to talk to our prisoner."

So much for gratitude. "I have evidence of illegal activity in those tunnels to hand to the police. I took photos—"

"Bring them later," she interrupted. "After the questioning is complete."

Why isn't she talking to the vampire? Had Drew excluded

her from the questioning? He might have, given her general lack of respect towards him, and the thought was amusing enough to banish my desire to fight her on that one. "I'll do that."

As I left, I spied my brother drifting in the opposite direction. "Mart—where are you going this time?"

"To taunt the vampire."

"Please don't," I said to him. "If Drew and the others are questioning him, you'll only cause the prisoner to clam up and stop talking."

"Doesn't sound like he's doing much talking in the first place." But he obeyed and followed me out of the police station, watched by an irate Petra. She hadn't commented on me having a conversation with thin air, but I'd bet she was filing it away alongside the many other strikes against me.

I messaged Drew telling him about Petra's rejection while we headed back to the inn, but I didn't expect him to be able to reply until he'd finished questioning the vampire.

Back at the inn, but Allie took one look at my bloodied arm and insisted that I should take the day off.

"I don't mind working," I protested. "I've got nothing else to do until the police let me come back and talk to the prisoner."

"Talk to the prisoner?" Carey looked up from where she sat at her usual table near the bar. "That's not your job, is it?"

"Nope, but I know vampires can be slippery. I can guarantee he'll try to make a break for it at some point, and I'd rather learn what he knows before then."

"Doesn't sound like you have much faith in Drew," Mart commented.

"Oi," I said. "It's Petra and the others I have no faith in, and to be honest, I have to wonder if the vampire was *trying* to get caught."

"Why would he do that?" Jia asked. "He's been trying to

avoid attention before now, hasn't he? Stealing blood samples instead of biting the locals…"

"Really?" Carey shuddered. "That's horrible."

"Better than him feeding on random passersby," I said firmly. "It's bad enough that he tried to take a bite out of me. I probably tasted terrible."

"Don't joke about that, Maura," Carey said. "You could have been killed."

"Indestructible Reaper, remember?" In truth, I didn't know if I *could* survive having my throat ripped out. Most likely not. "I wonder what would have happened if I'd accidentally dropped him in the afterworld."

"There's still time to do that," Mart reminded me.

"I might, if he does try to escape." Seeing Carey and Allie's confusion at the one-sided conversation, I added, "I'll have to wait and see if the police let me come back. You'd think Petra would have been a little more grateful for helping them out."

I went upstairs to change out of my damp and bloodied clothes before firing off an email to the police with the photos of the tunnel wall attached. Then I backed them up for good measure, being all too aware of Mina Devlin's penchant for deleting evidence.

We'd almost had her this time, but why had she hired a vampire to skulk around the tunnels? And how had he bypassed the coven's security to get into her office? He'd have needed to steal the key—though that wasn't impossible, given his speed and stealth—unless she'd given him one of her own.

If she had, it seemed an odd choice on her part to trust a vampire and not a witch, though it was possibly even more unusual for a vampire to choose to help a witch rise to power and not himself. Unless he was using her in some manner— or the other way around.

10

It was late afternoon when Drew finally messaged me and said I could come and talk to the vampire in the jail. I assumed he'd finally talked sense into Petra and the others, but a little gratitude on her part wouldn't have gone amiss.

I had to stop Mart from bringing the inflatable pumpkin along with him when he followed me across the bridge. I was starting to wish I'd gone back into the tunnel for another look around, but Drew said his officers were still poking around the other entrance. I didn't need to get myself into any more trouble with the authorities.

Drew met me at the door to the police station. "Sorry about earlier. I didn't know Petra would kick up that much of a fuss about you coming to the questioning."

"I hope Petra's about to grovel to me," I muttered. "Not only did I catch the vampire, but I also proved that I wasn't the person who broke into the prison last night."

"I had a word with her," he said, "but I'm afraid our prisoner isn't being very cooperative. I'm not sure he'll talk to you."

"He might talk to *me.*" Mart drifted ahead of me through the wall without asking for permission. Typical.

I followed Drew into the reception area, only to come to a halt when I spied Petra watching from near the door to the jail. She hadn't seen my brother, of course, but she didn't look any more contrite than she had earlier.

"You're back already?" she said. "I do hope you've thought carefully about your decisions, Reaper."

"I caught your vampire," I pointed out. "Also, I sent over a bunch of photos of the tunnel walls, if you're looking for proof someone was up to dodgy magic down there."

"Yes—I've got my team looking at those," Drew added. "Petra, I did say you could go home, didn't I?"

Petra's eyes narrowed. "I do find it interesting how easily you were able to overlook my order to stay away from those tunnels, Reaper."

"I gave her permission to go in there myself, Petra," Drew reprimanded. "Besides, these photos are certainly proof of illicit activity. If you want to find someone to punish for trespassing, I'd suggest you join the team examining the pictures and working out exactly what spell they were casting."

"There were also bodies in there." I hadn't had the chance to look around properly, but I remembered the neglected skeletons lying on the floor from my previous visit.

Petra's jaw twitched. "Unfortunates who died in the floods, no doubt."

"Why would anyone have voluntarily gone into tunnels under the river while it was flooding?" I was close to spilling the secret I'd kept even from Drew, but at this rate, the truth would explode publicly before anyone could be prepared for the fallout. "Those tunnels have been sealed off for years by someone who didn't want anyone going in."

"Yes, so you keep claiming." Petra remained unimpressed.

Why wouldn't she get out of the way of the door? "Can I get into the jail? I'd like to have a word with our vampire myself."

"Petra," Drew said in warning tones, "let Maura in, or I'll have to discipline you."

With visible reluctance, Petra stepped aside. As I moved towards the door, she said, "I do hope this isn't another false alarm. The last person you caught trespassing turned out to be innocent, didn't she?"

"That's up to the coven leader, not me." I'd forgotten about Priscilla. If she was still in jail, I expected Jennifer would ask for her to be freed soon, but no doubt she was a little distracted by the latest developments.

Drew walked behind me into the jail, closing the door behind us. "You shouldn't bait her, Maura."

"She's a grown adult police officer, not a rabid hellbeast," I said. "Some people need to get a life."

On the way through the holding cells, I spotted Priscilla staring at the wall. She didn't seem to have noticed my brother circling her, pulling faces and doing silly dances.

"Mart, cut that out," I told him. "Priscilla?"

She finally noticed me. "Maura. I heard you caught the vampire. Impressive."

"Erm… thanks?" Was her praise genuine? I couldn't tell. "You didn't steal the book, did you? It was him."

"I did try to tell you." She fidgeted with her sleeve. "Is Jennifer coming to let me out?"

"Ah… she's busy, but I expect she'll come here soon." Unless it turned out Priscilla had been working with the vampire after all, but I didn't know her well enough to make a judgement call. That part would be up to Jennifer.

I left the subdued witch and continued into the main part of the jail. Drew indicated the corridor ahead, where my gaze picked out the vampire's pale face pressed against the bars of his cell.

"You." The vampire bared his teeth in a grin. "I wondered if the police would send you next."

"They didn't. I sent myself." I tensed when he moved back fast—far quicker than a human—and folded his arms over his chest. "Any reason you've been hiding in a tunnel for weeks?"

Instead of answering, he watched my brother join me. "I'm surprised your sister lets you have so much freedom. She must know what the Reaper Council would do to you if you were discovered."

My blood iced over. "He's a ghost. They aren't illegal."

"He's no ordinary ghost." He gave me a smile. "It's not that much of a secret, Maura."

He knows. "Mina told you that, did she?"

Mina shouldn't have known, either, but she'd been obsessed with me for long enough that she might have worked it out. Still, if she'd been telling her followers I'd illegally raised my brother from death… *dammit.*

His grin intensified. "Now, that would be telling."

"You weren't so talkative earlier." I took a step closer to the bars to prove his fangs didn't intimidate me, ignoring my arm's continued throbbing. "Care to tell me why you decided to hang out in a damp tunnel for days or weeks? Except when you emerged to commit robbery?"

"Rather than wasting your time with me, you might want to look closer to home."

"What does that mean?" I tensed, my arm giving a sharp throb. "You have more of your vampy friends hiding down there in the tunnels, do you?"

Surely not. Vampires were loners, and it was unlikely enough that Mina had hired *one* vampire to work for her, let alone several.

When he didn't answer, I pushed on. "Was that where you hid the book?"

He simply laughed. "Witches have a knack for not seeing what's right in front of their faces."

So much for him being talkative. Granted, that's not the same as cooperative.

"Are you working with Priscilla?" I asked. "Or is she an unlucky bystander?"

He laughed again, which only added fuel to my temper. I moved closer to the bars and hissed, "Do you *want* to be here?"

"I have to admit, this place is preferable to a damp tunnel."

"Meaning yes?" *Had* he let himself get caught on purpose? "You must be really devoted to Mina to let her send you to scuttle around in the dark and then get arrested. Are you sure she'll come back to bail you out rather than letting you rot in a cell?"

Some of the mirth faded from his expression. "Careful, Reaper. It'd be a pity if you were to die before the real fun started."

"Fun?" Mart interjected. "What're you planning to do? Throw a party?"

The vampire ignored him. "Soon you'll come to see that even a Reaper isn't invulnerable, Maura... but I'm tired of talking to you."

He glided to the bench inside his cell and sat down, giving a clear indication that he wouldn't say another word. *Fine, then.* I looked for Drew and saw he'd walked off.

"He's talking to that Petra," Mart said to me. "I think she wants in."

"Will she ever quit?" Disgruntled, I scanned the nearby cells and spied Debora Rowe watching me from behind bars. Ah, screw it. I might as well talk to the others while I was here.

"Hey, there." I walked up to her cell. "I don't suppose you knew we had a vampire sniffing around town?"

"What do you think?" She laughed. "Got under your skin, did he?"

"Not in the slightest. Unless you count when he bit me, but that doesn't work on Reapers." I gritted my teeth when my arm gave another throb. "If he thinks he's going to get luxury treatment here, he's mistaken."

"Oh, he knows."

I caught the meaningful note in her voice. "Has he been sneaking in here and paying you visits? Giving updates on your leader's movements?"

If he'd broken into the police station, he'd certainly have been able to get into the jail as well... but what had he been doing? Plotting another breakout, or just giving the prisoners an insight into Mina's activities?

"Does it matter if he has?"

"I guess not." If Mina intended to have her allies escape, it would hardly be the first time. "I'd like to know where he hid the book, though."

"Oh, yes, the infamous book." She looked amused. "Did Jennifer tell you what it contains, exactly? Or is she still keeping you in the dark?"

What does that mean? She'd told me it contained illegal magic, which... Yeah, it wasn't that specific, but I could fill in the blanks with relative ease. "Is Priscilla working with you too? Or not?"

Another laugh. "Now, I'll let you decide that for yourself."

"It's up to Jennifer, not me." I'd had about enough of her taunting, but like with the vampire, there wasn't much I could do to loosen her tongue. I expected even Drew would reprimand me if I tried getting her to spill her secrets by pulling her into the afterworld to freak her out. "One of us is behind bars, and it's not me."

I walked away before she could irritate me even further, while Mart flipped her off. "Should I stay here and haunt them?"

"Tempting, but they're not worth it," I told him. "That includes the vampire."

"He deserves worse."

My steps faltered. It'd slipped my mind that the vampire might have been the one who'd tried to drown me. If he'd been a wizard in life, he might have retained the ability to activate the spells on the walls and seal the place off, even if he hadn't actually cast the spells himself... which might explain why I'd never seen the person responsible when I'd been in the tunnels. He'd have been able to get out of there easily and quickly enough to avoid being caught in the back-lash when the tunnels flooded—leaving Perry and me to drown.

I clenched my fists. "He does, but that's not my job."

When I walked past the holding cells on the way out, Priscilla called to me. "Can't you talk to Jennifer and ask her to get me out? She seems to respect you."

"I can't do that if she thinks you're guilty." I came to a halt outside her cell. "Out of interest, why *did* you come back to town at this precise moment?"

"For work, I told you," she said. "I got hired on for a temporary thing a few months ago. That was why I left."

"I assume you can provide references?"

"Yes." She didn't quite meet my eyes. "Look, I'm not the one who stole from the coven. You already caught him."

"If you're hiding more secrets, it's not my problem if they refuse to give you your freedom." I walked out into the police-station lobby and found Drew waiting for me. Petra must have finally taken the hint and left, so he was mercifully alone. "Priscilla wants out."

"I know she does," he said, "but I can't do anything until Jennifer comes in and withdraws the charges against her."

"If you find the book, it'll prove she isn't the thief." Irritation prickled beneath my skin. "Is your team still looking around the tunnels?"

"Yes, they're searching," Drew replied. "I'll let you know if we find anything else."

"No." Petra stepped out of a nearby office. "You aren't part of the investigation, Reaper."

Go away. "Yes, I am. *You* aren't, so—"

"Maura." Sensing my rising temper, Drew stepped in. "Petra, I told you to get your things and go home."

"Are you trying to get yourself fired?" I asked her. "Because I'll be enthusiastically cheering that on."

"Your influence over our supposed head of police is unacceptable," she said, eyeing Drew. "I'm not the only person who thinks it's compromising his ability to do his job."

"I think your grudge against me is compromising *your* ability to do your job," I said. "If you want to help in the investigation, why not volunteer as part of the team that's searching the tunnels?"

"That's right," Mart put in. "Maybe if we're really lucky, someone will shut you in."

"We already have the proof of illicit activity in the tunnels," Petra said. "We have the culprit, too, and yet you still won't leave us alone."

"You think the vampire carved those glyphs into the walls?" I guessed. "He's undead. He can't use magic, not the way a wizard can."

"Nevertheless."

My hands curled into fists. "If you want a second opinion, maybe you should call the Wardens again."

I'd never called her out as being responsible for that the

first time around, and from the way her eyes widened, she hadn't expected me to.

Drew cleared his throat. "The Wardens backed up Maura's words, Petra. You know they did. You've stepped too far."

Petra was silent for an instant. "Everything I do is for the safety of this town and its people."

I knew better, but I still said, "I should hope so." She was more fixated on her own advancement and on undermining Drew because of her irrational grudge against me. "A vampire running amok is dangerous for the people of the town too. Especially one who just hinted that he's planning a breakout, along with Mina's other allies. So, you know, maybe focus on that."

"I will," Drew interjected. "Maura—I'll talk to you later, okay?"

From his worried frown, he wanted to say more but not in front of Petra. Which was fine by me. I'd had quite enough passive-aggressive nonsense for one day.

But I had one last stop to make on the way back to the inn. When I walked towards the cemetery, Mart groaned. "Not old Harold again. Didn't he shut us out last time?"

"I figured he might want to know we caught the vampire."

I knocked twice before the old Reaper pulled open the door. "Yes?"

I was so disarmed by him actually answering the door that my mind went temporarily blank. "Erm… I caught the vampire."

"Shouldn't you be telling the police, not me?"

"I did." That was more in character for the grumpy Reaper. "He's in jail, but I thought you might want to know that he turned out to be hiding in the tunnels."

He tutted at me. "You took the police in there? You never listen to anyone, do you?"

Now he sounded like the Reaper I was used to. "I didn't take them in there, but they haven't found the book yet, so it won't be the last time."

"Haven't they?" His tone sharpened. "Then they'd better look harder."

"Nobody is being very specific about why the book is so dangerous," I said. "What exactly does it contain instructions on? Necromancy is a pretty broad area."

"You have the imagination and training not to need it spelled out, don't you?"

"Demons?" I guessed. "Mass summonings? Jennifer's looking at the photos I sent of the actual glyphs, but—"

"You took photos of them?" His jaw twitched. "Do you *want* everyone to know how to cast those spells?"

"I only gave them to the police and the head of the coven," I said defensively. "And Mina already knows, doesn't she?"

He grunted. "If you aren't careful, you're going to get more people killed with your foolishness."

"I thought you wanted evidence out there," I said. "Evidence that Mina was casting illegal spells in the tunnels."

"I never said I wanted the whole magical world to know."

"Isn't it better than nobody knowing at all?" He of all people ought to be able to see that. "It's done now. We caught the vampire."

"If you want to be congratulated, you're asking the wrong person."

"I'm aware of that." I cast around in my mind for anything else pertinent that he might need to know. "The vampire knew what I did to my brother. That I bound him to me. I don't know how he found out, but I guess Mina is telling people."

"Again—I warned you." He gave me a flinty stare. "If she could tell the Reaper Council without exposing herself, she certainly would."

Dread gripped my chest. "Good job she's a wanted criminal, then."

What about my dad, though? My suspicions as to why he'd called the inn remained, but as yet, there was nothing to connect the vampire we'd caught with the strange timing of my Reaper father's attempt to get in touch with his one surviving child.

Soon you'll come to see that even a Reaper isn't invulnerable, Maura...

If the vampire was the one who'd trapped me in the tunnel, he knew I was fully aware of that fact. But what if he hadn't meant me—a half Reaper—but an *actual* Reaper? Like my dad?

I took in a breath. "Harold, what aren't you telling me about this book? Are there spells in there that are deadly even to Reapers?"

I swore he *rolled his eyes* at me. "You are truly the densest Reaper I've ever met."

He closed the door in my face without another word, and I rocked back on my heels, my arm throbbing again.

"That means yes," I murmured to my brother. "Mina's not trying to threaten the *Reapers*… is she?"

"She has more sense," Mart said, his voice devoid of its usual humour. "She wouldn't attack the council."

But what about a lone Reaper? Like Shelton... or my dad?

11

One ghost tour later, a very apologetic Drew showed up at the inn. My mood improved immeasurably when he came to rescue me from the usual post-tour questions from the guests, and we sought sanctuary in my room.

The ghost tour had been fun, but the vampire remained on my mind, along with my conversation with the Reaper. It didn't help that the police had yet to find the missing book despite extensive searching.

"We have photos of all the glyphs on the walls," Drew told me. "And we removed some of the bones we found down there for forensic testing too."

"Good," I said, though a thrill of dread raced through my nerves at the thought of how the unfortunate former owners of those bones might have met their end. "They're old, so I guess it'll be hard to figure out the cause of death."

"That was what I thought, but it's worth looking into," he said. "If we can identify them, we might be able to work out if they were coven members or if they were listed as missing during the floods."

"Yeah." We'd bring Mina to justice one way or another,

and yet... What if the vampire's taunts hadn't just been taunts? "Better focus on the vampire for now. I don't like that he was probably visiting the prisoners behind your back."

"Neither do I." He sat down on my bed, looking as tired as I felt. "He was damned *fast*—and stronger than I expected."

"Same," I said. "I only got him because I dragged him into the afterworld, but I guess it'd cause you a bunch of inconvenient paperwork if I took him in there for more questioning."

"Maura."

"Joking, joking." I kicked off my shoes and sat on the bed alongside him. "In all seriousness, though, we need to find where he hid that book. The Reaper implied... He implied the spells inside its pages could harm even a Reaper."

If it was true, that was bad news for more than my own immediate family.

"We'll find it," Drew said firmly. "The vampire is all talk. He'll want to make it seem as if he's had this master plan from the start, when the reality is that he was careless and got caught."

"I don't know," I said. "He seemed pretty confident, and I don't like that he knew what I did to my brother."

"Mina's doing, I expect," he said. "Relax. He's in jail, and I'll send another team down into the tunnels first thing in the morning."

"What if he's hidden the book somewhere else?" Maybe that was his plan to win his freedom. If he offered to trade the book in exchange, the police wouldn't go for it, but— wait. "Or what if he already gave it to Mina?" Chills scurried down my arms.

Drew shook his head. "No. I've had people watching the area for any signs of her. Including the other tunnel entrance."

"Good." Yet I couldn't shake off my worries that we were

playing into the enemy's hands no matter what we did. "It's just… weird. My dad's call yesterday and now the news that this book might be a legitimate threat to the Reapers…"

He stiffened. "That seems unlikely."

"For anyone except her, I'd agree." I gave a shudder. "Maybe she's been poking around my history as much as I've been poking into hers. There aren't *that* many independent Reapers who ditched their apprenticeships."

"I thought it was nearly impossible for regular humans to get hold of that information."

"So did I." I'd also forgotten how much I'd told Drew about the Reapers, come to that. "But you know Mina. She'll go to any lengths for an edge over me."

"I thought you said the Reapers were invincible. Are you sure our prisoner isn't trying to goad you into leaving Hawkwood Hollow at a time of crisis?"

"What—going home to Greenwood Lake?" I hadn't yet voiced the name of my former home in front of Drew, and it felt rusty in my mouth, underused. "The thought crossed my mind, but honestly, with my Reaper abilities, I can get there and back fast enough that it wouldn't be an issue."

"You can," he agreed, "but I don't like the timing of this."

Neither did I, but what if my hunch was right? Shelton wasn't supposed to have gotten in touch with my dad, and if Mina genuinely intended to strike at my old home while everyone was distracted…

I took in a breath. "I'll call my dad again first. Ask him some more questions."

"Do that." Drew reached for me, pulled me into an embrace. "Mina's trying to make you paranoid, I bet."

"She might be, but old Harold isn't helping matters. Neither is the vampire, despite being in jail." It'd help if I was confident that he'd *stay* there.

"No." He ran his hand down the side of my face, cupped

my chin, and kissed me. "Come on, Maura. Don't let Mina and that vampire make you doubt yourself."

"I don't doubt myself. I doubt *them*." I kissed him back. "Trust me, I'm fully confident in my ability to kick the crap out of them."

He laughed. "That's what I love about you."

Love. My heart stuttered. He'd never used that word with me before. Sensing my hesitation, he pulled back from me, his gaze searching. "Maura? Are you here?"

"Yeah." I kissed him again, pushed him down onto the bed. "I'm here."

And I'll die before I let Mina take you away from me.

―――

My brother was less than enthused about my plan when I tracked him down in the games room early the following morning. I'd woken at dawn and was unable to fall back asleep. "You want to call home again? Didn't you already make your answer clear?"

"I did, but that was before I found out Mina's book of dark magic might be a threat even to a Reaper." I stifled a yawn behind my hand. I'd left Drew sleeping, not wanting to disturb him, but our pleasant date night hadn't erased my suspicions concerning Mina and her possible antics at my old home.

"You think our evil ex-coven leader wants to threaten the *council?*" Mart gave a loud laugh that didn't ring true. "Yeah, no. She doesn't have a death wish."

"She doesn't mind sacrificing a few followers," I said. "I never said she wanted to threaten the council, just a Reaper. A powerful demon could give a lone Reaper a run for their money, and both Dad and Shelton fall into that category."

"Her most loyal followers are locked up," said Mart. "I bet

the vampire wants you to look the other way while he instigates another breakout. He and the others are trying to distract you."

"It was old Harold who knew what was in that book," I said. "He was the one who gave me the idea. You heard him."

"Dad didn't mention Mina at all, did he?"

"No, but would he admit to being threatened by a mere witch? Would Shelton?" The fact that he'd called me at all was proof enough that something was wrong.

"No." He gave a snort. "No, he'd stab it with his scythe."

"Maura," Drew said, pushing open the games-room door. "Sorry—I've got to run. The witches have shown up at the jail."

"The… witches?" My heart dropped. "Not Mina's allies?"

"No." He backed out into the lobby. "The coven leader. And guess which officer was there to greet her?"

"Petra." I groaned and walked after him across the lobby. "Why on earth did Jennifer want to go there in the early hours of the morning? Not to set Priscilla free, I assume."

Was there another break-in?

"She didn't say." Drew led the way out the automatic doors, and we walked across the bridge towards the centre of Hawkwood Hollow. If there'd been another break-in, it must have been one of Mina's allies, but with the vampire in jail, who else was in the area?

When we neared the high street, I spied Priscilla walking out of the jail, escorted by Jennifer Ness herself. Frowning, Drew strode over to catch up to them. "What's going on?"

"My apologies for overstepping," Jennifer said in tones that suggested she wasn't particularly sorry. "I was told your team intended to let my coven member out of confinement, so I decided to expedite the process."

"That wasn't your job." I could hear Drew struggling to

keep a polite tone. "Who exactly let her out of the holding cells?"

I was willing to bet I knew. "Petra. You know she's deliberately trying to undermine Drew's authority, don't you?"

"Priscilla has a confession to make to me," said Jennifer, apparently ignoring my comment. "You're welcome to come and listen, Maura."

"What?" My heart skipped a beat. "By 'confession,' I assume you don't mean the sort that has to be kept to a police record?"

"I mean she intends to admit why she came back to town." Jennifer gave Priscilla a nudge. "We're going back to the coven headquarters."

Conflicted, I watched the pair of them cross the road. "I should…"

"Follow them," Drew said to me. "I'm going to have a word with my officers."

Oh boy. Hoping he gave Petra a stern talking-to, I ran after the witches and into the coven headquarters.

To my surprise, Wendy was back, looking none the worse for wear after her time out of the action. She wrung her hands when she saw me enter. "Oh no. Not you."

"Nice to see you too," I replied. "Jennifer invited me."

I assumed the coven leader had asked her assistant to attend the questioning as well because Wendy tailed me upstairs to Jennifer's office.

"Well?" Jennifer seated herself behind the desk as the three of us arranged ourselves in front. "Priscilla, you said you had some information?"

Priscilla glanced at me. "Does the Reaper have to be here?"

"She has a name," I said, "and yes, she does. I heard you had a confession to make. Did you steal the book?"

"No." She shook her head. "No. I didn't come here to steal from the coven either. I came to help."

"Enlighten me," said Jennifer. "You must know you've behaved in a manner that implicates you in the actions of those who want to unseat me from my position."

"Not me." She took in a measured breath. "No. I—the truth is, I came here because I knew the tunnels had been discovered again."

"You knew?" I tried to read her expression, but her attention was on the coven leader. "By 'again,' you mean you knew Mina kept them hidden to avoid anyone else discovering their existence, didn't you? How long were you aware of them?"

"I suspected they existed, but I could never find their location when I was here," she said. "I'm not the only one, but Mina's far more powerful than the rest of us, and even when I left town, her closest coven members walked free. I didn't dare return until they were behind bars."

That sounds familiar. Jia had a similar story, except she'd left years ago, not after Mina had already been ousted. "You know, I'm not sure I believe you."

"Maura," Jennifer said, "I believe I am the one conducting this questioning."

"I know," I said impatiently, "but do you think she's telling the truth? She left town after Mina already ran."

"I knew leaving beforehand would see me exiled from the coven for life," Priscilla said haltingly. "And because…"

"Yes?" Jennifer prompted.

"Because some of us wanted to keep an eye on her."

"On Mina." Jennifer's eyes narrowed. "You knew where she was hiding?"

"No, of course not," said Priscilla. "She's been moving between hiding places, which makes her very difficult to track. We've been trying, though."

"Who is 'we'?" Jennifer enquired.

"Former coven members." Her gaze flickered towards me then Wendy. "I don't want to mention their names in front of witnesses. They already fear for their lives."

"Any enemy of Mina's is safe with the coven," Jennifer told her. "But go on. What drove you to come back?"

"The vampire." Priscilla lifted her chin. "I was hunting him down. I was sent to follow him and keep an eye on his movements."

"Have *you* been in the tunnels?" I couldn't help asking. "Why not hand him over to the police yourself?"

"He's a vampire," she said. "The only way to catch a vampire is through trickery or an accident—or if he intentionally lets himself get caught."

I stiffened at the implication.

"He certainly wanted *my* attention," Jennifer said. "Why does Mina Devlin have a vampire doing her bidding?"

"I'm not exactly sure, but the vampire is a rogue with an arrest warrant on his head," Priscilla said. "The Wardens have been searching for him for weeks. Even the Reaper Council are aware of him."

The Reaper Council?

A horrible suspicion seized hold of me. "Do any of these people need to be notified that he's been caught?"

If the Reaper Council deemed the vampire a big enough threat to come and get him in person...

"Maura." Jennifer eyed me. "Was there something you wanted to say?"

"Only that Mina Devlin would absolutely love it if the Wardens and the Reaper Council all descended upon Hawkwood Hollow at once."

"Really." Jennifer studied me. "You believe she'd use the other Reapers against you?"

"Is there anything she *wouldn't* do?" Priscilla didn't have a clue, and neither did Wendy, but I'd have thought Jennifer Ness would know how far the former coven leader would go to run me out of town. "I'm going to have to talk to the police about this one."

Unfortunately, Petra had clearly woken up ready to fight that morning, and the police were also supposed to be sending another team into the tunnels to find that book. I didn't want to miss out on the rest of Priscilla's questioning, but every minute the vampire was here in town risked the Reaper Council or the Wardens showing up to collect him. If they did have a warrant out for him, they'd likely send a single person to hunt for him first—like Shelton.

I left Jennifer's office, jogged downstairs, and paused to assess my options as the door to the witches' headquarters closed behind me. Unfortunately, the best person to talk to about all things Reaper Council was old Harold himself, and he'd been downright maddening yesterday.

Drew was probably still dealing with Petra's little rebellion, so I messaged him and began to walk resignedly to the Reaper's cottage.

When I reached the cemetery, I did a double take when I saw old Harold already waiting outside.

"I should have known to expect a visit from you," he said.

"Why?" Tension zipped up my spine. "Did you hear from the Reaper Council?"

"What?" He scowled. "No. What've you done now?"

"Not me. That vampire? Turns out he's a wanted rogue."

"Of course he is." Harold swore under his breath. "Only you could bring a rogue vampire here."

"He was already here." I'd had about enough of the old Reaper flinging blame in my direction. "We'd have found him sooner if you hadn't decided to hold your tongue about that missing book."

"Better to keep silent than rampage around like a wild manticore."

"You don't want that book falling into the wrong hands, do you?" Frankly, his attitude was giving me a headache. "Look, we have a situation. If the Reaper Council sends someone to retrieve our vampire, the first thing they'll do is report this town's existence and probably shut down the inn."

"You're telling me what I already know," the Reaper said. "You should have dealt with the vampire yourself, not entrusted him to the authorities."

"What, left him in the afterworld?" If I'd had a scythe, I'd have been able to do worse, but I'd never Reaped the soul of a vampire before. By all accounts, they were incredibly tough for even a Reaper to kill.

He scoffed. "Any other Reaper wouldn't have hesitated."

"You think I should have disobeyed the law and proved Petra right?" I had to admit that the notion of borrowing Harold's scythe and leaping into the jail to finish the vampire off wasn't unappealing. "Even if the vamp was dead, the council would keep searching for him until they found answers. You're the one with the contacts, so it'd be very much appreciated if you could call Shelton and explain."

"Your Warden friends left you their number, didn't they?"

Oh. Right. "I can't guarantee they'd be free to come here themselves, at least not right away."

"That's your problem," he said. "Don't you have another Reaper you can contact?"

"My dad." Crap. If I called him back... Well, I'd have to figure out how to explain why I wanted to know if the Reaper Council had put out an arrest warrant for any vampires recently. But it was still better than trying to rely on old Harold to do something useful for once. "Fine. Have it your way."

I pulled out my phone and typed in my dad's number from memory. I'd been meaning to make the call anyway, but I couldn't suppress my suspicion that Mina was playing with all of us like pieces on a chessboard.

Never play chess with a Reaper. We're sore losers.

I hit the call button before I could change my mind. My heart thumped in my ears while the phone rang a couple of times then went straight to a dial tone.

I tried again. And again. No answer came, though I retyped the number as I walked in case I'd gotten it wrong the first time. My dad might be out on a mission or just out of the house without access to a phone. There was no reason to panic... yet.

"Mart," I called out as I ran into the inn's lobby, past a startled Allie. "Where are you?"

"Here." He zipped into view. "What's up with you?"

I beckoned him into the games room and lowered my voice. "I can't get through to Dad on the phone."

"So?" He floated behind me into the room. "Obviously, he's out. Why would that be a problem?"

"The Reaper Council has an arrest warrant out for that vampire," I murmured, conscious that the other ghosts had gathered around the TV at the back of the games room. "I have a feeling he's been trying to bait them."

"Scumbag," Mart said. "Can't you ask your Reaper friend to call the council himself and fob them off with an excuse?"

"I already asked."

"I can be more persuasive than you," he said. "I'll hang around annoying him all day until he caves in."

"Nobody can stop the Reaper Council, Mart," I whispered. "You know that. Harold won't be able to keep them out."

"Where's that detective of yours, then?"

"Arguing with Petra," I said. "She decided to take matters

into her own hands and set that witch free—you know, Priscilla. Turns out she was chasing the vampire, not working with him."

"Then ask her to escort him to the Reaper Council herself."

"Not sure that'll go over well." The vampire, unlike Priscilla, was still behind bars, and the police wouldn't want me setting their prisoner free. Drew didn't need me complicating matters any further than they already were. "I can call the Wardens, but it's anyone's guess as to whether they'd want to come to the other side of the country for this."

"If anything, you owe *them* a favour for saving your life. What're you all looking at?"

I raised my head to see who he was addressing and saw that all the other ghosts were watching the pair of us from in front of the TV.

Vicky spoke first. "Are the Reaper Council coming here?"

"Absolutely not." In an effort to keep the human occupants of the inn from overhearing our conversation, I'd unintentionally terrified the ghostly ones. *Great job, Maura.* "They wouldn't send more than one person to retrieve a single vampire. I'll deal with—"

Someone rapped on the door then nudged it open. "Someone's here for you, Maura," Allie called from outside the room.

"Huh?" I stepped out into the lobby to the slightly alarming sight of old Harold the Reaper standing at the foot of the stairs. "Erm... hi?"

"Outside," he growled without preamble.

Too baffled to argue, I walked out of the inn with my brother drifting behind me. "Did you follow us?"

"No," he said over his shoulder. "I called Shelton, and he said that your father was sent on a mission."

"Why…?" Harold had come over here to tell me that? Unless… "What mission?"

"A bounty," he said. "I think you can guess which vampire it was for."

"What?" Alarm blared through my mind. "You can't be serious."

My dad was coming here, and my new life was about to blow sky-high.

12

I took off for the police station first, calling Drew as I left. He picked up right away to my relief. "Maura? Are you all right?"

"No. Drew, he's coming here."

"Who?" I heard the confusion in his voice. "Who's coming?"

"My dad." I clenched my hand around the phone. "Acting on the Reaper Council's authority. He's going to come for the vampire, and…"

And in the process, he'd find out the town was flooded with ghosts. The vampire would become the least of his concerns, and it wouldn't surprise me if he acted there and then to report the town to the Reaper Council. In the ensuing confusion, Mina Devlin would doubtless find a way to take advantage of everyone's distraction. Honestly, it was kind of ingenious of her to plan to have my own family turn me in to the authorities.

Drew swore under his breath. "Is there any way you can find him first?"

"Possibly." My Reaper abilities would enable me to track

down another Reaper, but the real question was whether I'd be able to convince him not to report Hawkwood Hollow. If I took Mart with me, it might help… or not. Either way, I couldn't leave my brother behind. He deserved to be in on this too.

"All right." Drew took in a breath. "I'll tell my officers there might be someone coming to pick up the vampire soon. I can contact the Wardens, too, if that helps."

"All right. I'll try to be fast, but—"

"Don't waste any more time," Harold growled from behind me, having followed me out of the inn. "Your father was sent on the mission yesterday, so he already has a day's head start."

"Got it." To Drew, I added, "I'll let you know if there are any more developments, okay?"

"Of course." Worry filled his tone. "Are you sure there isn't anything I can do?"

"Keep an eye on that vampire." It wouldn't surprise me if he found a way to escape while everyone was distracted. "I'll see you later."

I ended the call before the emotions brimming inside me could break free. *I can't let this happen.* Drew wasn't the person most under threat from the Reaper Council finding out about the state of things here, but there were too many other people I wanted to protect, both living and dead.

"You're going to find our dad?" Mart floated over to me.

"You know I don't have a choice." I held out a hand. "Coming with me?"

"Obviously."

His ghostly hand slipped into mine, and we stepped into the afterworld.

The dark folded around us, and I could no longer see anything but utter blackness, save for Mart hovering at my side.

"What if *this* is the trap?" he suggested. "If we leave town, Mina might act."

"I know, but if I don't find him, Dad will show up at the inn first." I scanned the surrounding shadows for any sign of a scythe-wielding figure. "We'd both be out of a job, and I bet Mina would seize on the general confusion to stage a comeback."

"Do you think you can convince our dad that the ghosts *want* to stay here?"

"I can try." I focused on the darkness, seeing several glowing shapes nearby. Ghosts, of course. The number of spirits around us made it tricky to pinpoint a single person, and the shadowy form of old Harold didn't help matters. His presence chilled the whole area like an open refrigerator.

All right. I'd have to go farther from the town to stand a chance of finding another Reaper. "If I were Dad, I'd start from one of the normal towns nearby as a base. I'd prefer it if he was on the other side of the country instead, but I doubt we'll be that lucky."

"Obviously not." Mart snorted. "He's not here yet, though. We'd know."

"Then let's go." I leapt into the shadow and reappeared on a deserted country lane. Farther from Hawkwood Hollow, it was slightly easier to get my bearings. Mart hovered next to me while I turned on the spot, no longer able to sense the abundance of ghosts that flooded the village. But I also didn't sense the familiar icy cold nearness of another Reaper.

"Let's try this again." I stepped through the shadows and headed north this time, picking a direction at random.

"Not here either," Mart said when we emerged into an empty field. "Are we going to do this all day?"

"You're the one who wanted to come with me." Back into the afterworld I went before I unintentionally got myself chased off by a farmer for trespassing.

As the minutes passed with no sign of any other Reapers, I was just starting to dare to hope that my dad had somehow gone in the wrong direction and was wandering around the Highlands of Scotland or something.

Until a familiar chill rippled through the afterworld and brought me to a dead halt. Another Reaper.

Mart stiffened too. "It's him."

I spun on the spot, tracking the source of the unbearable coldness emanating from nearby.

"Mart," I whispered. "Get behind me. If he has his scythe, you don't want to be in the way."

"I'm not an imbecile." He moved close enough that his ghostly arm touched mine, but that chill was nothing compared to the one created by my dad's presence, like a black hole of utter darkness.

And here I was, about to jump into it.

Here we go.

Coldness enveloped me as if I'd fallen headfirst into a snowdrift, but the freezing sensation was immediately eclipsed by an all-encompassing dread when the darkness receded, and I found myself standing in front of a menacing hooded figure. He loomed over me, scythe in his hands, terrifying and ready to strike.

"Wait." I held up my hands, conscious of my brother cowering behind me. "It's just me, Dad."

"Maura." A familiar voice spoke from beneath the Reaper's hood, and he lowered the scythe. "I thought you didn't use your Reaper skills any longer."

"I don't normally, except in case of emergency."

"What emergency?" While I couldn't see his face, I could tell the moment his attention locked on my brother. "You..."

"Wait." I moved forward, as close to my dad as I could get without touching that sharp blade. "Put the scythe away. Mart and I are here to talk to you, nothing more."

"Must you keep breaking the rules?" He sighed, the sound surprisingly human, and lowered the scythe. With one hand, he pushed down his hood, revealing a weary face that was an older mirror of my own. "What exactly do you think constitutes an emergency?"

"Someone sending *you* on a false vampire hunt." I remained tense, conscious of the darkness of the afterworld surrounding us. "We already caught the vampire, and the Wardens are on their way to collect him."

I was stretching the truth a little, but I *had* intended to call the Wardens before old Harold had broken the news of my dad's mission and forced me to improvise, and Drew might have already done so.

"That wasn't what I was told." He searched my face. "What are you hiding?"

"Someone wants to set us against one another." There was no way to do this without revealing the truth, even if that was exactly what Mina Devlin wanted. "I made an enemy of a powerful coven leader who's been up to some seriously nefarious magic. She intentionally set the vampire loose in the area to target me, but I caught him first, so there's no need for—"

"If that's the case," he said, "I'll collect him myself."

"He's not the real danger," I said quickly. "You should know that the witch who sent the vampire after me should also have a warrant on her head for dabbling in illegal necromancy, and unlike him, she's still at large."

"We don't deal with witches." Shadows swept around his feet, warning me that he was about to jump through the afterworld again—and this time, he'd have a pretty good idea of where he was going.

"She summoned *demons*, Dad."

"Then why not call the council yourself?" A pause. "You're avoiding them."

"Of course I'm avoiding them." I gestured to my brother behind me. "Do you think they'd let this slide? They'd banish him from this world without a moment's hesitation."

"Would that be such a bad thing?"

"Hey!" Mart said indignantly. "I'm right here, you know."

"It's not right for ghosts to linger after their time." Dad's eyes were on me rather than on Mart, and his expression was wearier than ever. "Don't fight me on this, Maura. I let you leave home, and I refrained from reporting you to the council for keeping your Reaper abilities. Perhaps it was the wrong choice, but—"

"No, it was the right choice. There are some things the council doesn't understand," I said. "They're not human."

"Neither are you," he said. "You might have made your home among humans, but you're not one of them."

Okay, that was uncalled-for. "Where else am I supposed to go? The Reapers wouldn't take me—though I'd like to know why you changed your mind." He clearly wasn't under threat from Mina Devlin, but why had he called the inn in the first place?

"I acted hastily when I banished you," he said. "Shelton… He told me of you. He reminded me of how capable a Reaper you are."

My eyes stung. *Does he have to twist the knife in the wound?* "That was a long time ago."

"I know, but my point remains."

"I'm not coming home." I spoke firmly, despite the pain of the long-buried part of me who'd fought so hard for his approval as a child. "I have a new home, and I'm happy there —but someone is doing her best to ruin it for me. Someone the Reaper Council ought to have their attention on. I'm not joking when I say this witch is dangerous. I already told the Wardens that."

"The Wardens," he repeated. "You'd rather work with *them* than your own kind?"

"My own kind?" I echoed. "I might be half-Reaper, but it's a whole lot more complicated when you have a mortal life-span. Also, I'm not putting my brother at risk by contacting the council."

"I see." He still hadn't so much as looked at Mart. "I hoped the years had changed your mind, but I see I was mistaken."

"We've all changed. Well, some of us have." I felt kind of sorry for him in a way, for being too stubborn to see that Mart was still *here*. Not alive but as much a person as I was. "I meant it when I said I was happy with my new life."

"You're really content with running ghost tours?" He shook his head in incredulity. "Don't tell me you've picked up more strays."

"Erm." Now that he mentioned it, that was pretty much what I'd done.

"Maura," he said slowly, "if you're defying the council by sparing *more* ghosts from the afterworld, you're playing a dangerous game."

"I didn't bring them back." I should have known I wouldn't be able to dance around the truth forever, and in a way, it was a relief to speak plainly about Mina's crimes to someone who had the power to take her to account. Dad might not be the council's favourite Reaper, but he'd have an easier time handling them than Harold would, for one.

"Really." His tone was flat. "I have trouble believing that, Maura."

"Mart was an exception." Hurt crept into my voice, despite my best efforts. "You should know that."

Mart himself shifted behind me and whispered, "Don't tell him."

"He's going to figure it out anyway." I took in a breath and addressed Dad. "That witch I mentioned? She dabbled in necromancy and caused dozens of deaths, including the local Reaper's apprentice's. He went into early retirement as a result, and nobody has been able to prove she was responsible until now. I have proof—"

"That's quite enough." He held up a hand. "Am I right in thinking that instead of cleaning up the mess this neglectful Reaper created, you decided to… what, open a ghost-tour business?"

"That wasn't me," I said ineffectually. "I needed a job, and the ghosts aren't doing any harm."

"No harm?" he said. "If what you said is true—if what she did was dangerous enough to cause the death of a Reaper— Mina Devlin might well have destabilised the entire afterworld around the area. I have to see this for myself."

"No, you really don't." My hands clenched into fists. "You want the vampire? I'll bring him to you myself."

"I'm sorry, Maura, but it's my job to deal with this situation and report it to the council."

Well, I tried. If I couldn't make him see sense, I'd have to go with plan B.

My one advantage was that he hadn't actually set foot in Hawkwood Hollow yet. He might know it existed, but he hadn't seen the town with his own eyes, and even a Reaper needed to have some level of familiarity with a place to travel there through the afterworld.

"Have it your way, then." I spun on my heel and vanished into the shadows. As I did so, I whispered to Mart, "Go in the opposite direction. He's more likely to follow me than you, but just in case…"

As Mart vanished, my father the Reaper appeared in his place, fury etched on his face. Picturing a random location, I hopped through the shadows and emerged onto a street of startled shoppers. Hoping I hadn't unintentionally landed in a normal town and exposed the magical world for everyone to see, I turned back into the darkness and pictured a deserted country lane.

Out of the shadows I walked then back in, again and again—until I was dizzy enough that even *I* didn't have the faintest idea where I was. I staggered out onto a windy coastal cliff and stopped to catch my breath.

My phone buzzed with a call. I debated for a moment then answered, hearing Drew's muffled voice. "Maura, where are you?"

"Trying to stop my dad from showing up in town with a horde of Reapers," I told him. "He was sent after the vampire."

"The vampire's gone," said Drew. "You were right. He escaped, and he did a hell of a lot of damage in the process."

"No." My heart jumped in my chest. "What did he do?"

"He bit several of my officers." He swore under his breath. "It's my fault. I called the Wardens using the number you gave me, but they said they were tied up working on another case. While I was making the call, a group of rebellious officers decided to take matters into their own hands and escort the vampire to the local Wardens' branch in person."

"What?" My voice snapped out. "*Petra.* I thought you told her she was on her last warning."

"Oh, I did," he said grimly. "And she's thoroughly regretting her choice now. The trouble is, I'm not sure she'll live that long."

My mouth went dry. "Did the vampire bite her?"

"Yes. Several times."

Oh boy. She'd brought it on herself, but that didn't change how screwed we were now the vampire was loose. "Did the vampire run back to the tunnels, do you know?"

"My team is searching for him in there, but we believe he might have fled the town instead."

"I hope he has," I said fervently. "My dad was sent to bring him in, and if he finds Hawkwood Hollow, the vampire will drop way lower on his priority list."

Either way, a dangerous vampire on the loose was never good news, especially one with a murderous grudge against me and ties to Mina Devlin.

I guess we're going vampire hunting again.

13

There was a hitch. Before I could hop into the afterworld, my dad appeared at my side with an aggrieved expression on his face. "You can't lead me away from your home forever, Maura."

"Change of plans," I replied. "The vampire? He's escaped jail, bitten a bunch of people, and gone on the run. Want to help me find him?"

"Help you?" he echoed. "The vampire was *my* mission. I'll find him myself."

"Good luck with that." Crap. The vampire's escape wouldn't stop Dad from going into Hawkwood Hollow in search of the former prisoner. "You can't track him through the afterworld. That's why you've been walking in circles for the past day, isn't it?"

The Reaper narrowed his eyes at me. "I'll find him."

In a swirl of shadows, he was gone. I might have followed, but the vampire had unintentionally offered me a reprieve. If he *was* still hiding in Hawkwood Hollow, I had the chance to catch him before Dad showed up.

"There you are." Mart hopped out of the afterworld at my side. "Where'd Dad go?"

"After the vampire. He escaped jail, attacking Petra and some of the other officers in the process."

"Really?" Mart snickered. "First time he's done something useful. I should thank him."

"That's not going to deter Dad from coming to Hawkwood Hollow." I paced along the cliffside. "I think we can risk going back first, but it's not going to be easy to find the vampire unless he's in a really obvious place like the tunnels."

"Even if he is, you're right. Dear old Dad isn't going to quit the search now you've told him the truth."

Dammit. I couldn't tell every ghost to get out of town until he was gone, and besides, there was no hiding from a Reaper.

"I know." I called on the shadows. "But we have to stop that vampire before he causes even more damage."

We returned to Hawkwood Hollow in a single jump, landing next to the police station. Our appearance startled the hell out of a few shoppers, but not many people were outside—and it was obvious to see why. The police station doors lay wide open, and inside the lobby was a complete mess. Someone had flung a desk straight through a window, and broken glass littered the floor. I averted my gaze from the red smears on the wall and was relieved to see Drew didn't have a scratch on him.

"Maura." Drew strode over and embraced me. "Are you okay?"

"Yeah, but my dad's going to be coming here as soon as he figures out where I went." I glanced behind him at the blood-stained floor. "Where'd the vampire run off to?"

"I wish I knew," he said. "I had to help the officers he attacked. They're in the hospital, recovering."

"Petra's still alive?"

"Yes, but she's out for the count," he said. "I sent out two teams—one to the north, one to the tunnels—but the rest of us are stretched thin, and we also have to fix the damage to the office."

"And you never did find the book." There was a chance the vampire might come back to retrieve it, but he'd already succeeded in drawing the attention of the Reapers. Mina would have plenty of opportunities to get hold of the book in the ensuing chaos—unless I stopped her.

"No," he said. "Jennifer is displeased at the lack of results, but we searched the tunnel as thoroughly as possible."

"Despite certain members of your own team getting underfoot," I added. "If the book *is* in the tunnel, I wouldn't be surprised if that was where the vampire went, but there are no guarantees that he'll make it easy to find him."

"And—the Reaper?" Drew eyed me in concern. "You said he was coming here. Does that mean he's bringing the council?"

"It might." The weight of my failure fell on me like an anvil. If I'd just waited a short while longer until the vampire escaped again, I wouldn't have been in this mess. "He insisted he'd have to come and look for himself, but I don't know if he'll bring the council along too. Either way, old Harold is going to kill me."

"Yes, he is," said Mart. "Well done."

My hands clenched. "I didn't see another option. He already figured out I was hiding ghosts at the inn for the purposes of running tours, and it's not like he was unaware of how I brought Mart back from the afterworld."

Drew grimaced. "Is there anything I can do?"

"No... Well, I don't know," I backtracked. "Find the vampire. No, find the book. That's what Mina wants, and unlike the vampire, the Reaper Council has no idea it exists."

My dad didn't even want to know, but he might listen to another Reaper.

Drew and I parted ways, and I reluctantly left the police station for the cemetery. Mart flew alongside me, and I took a moment before I spoke to him. "I'm sorry. I should've guessed Dad would have stayed set in his ways. I won't let him hurt you or the other ghosts."

"You can't protect all of us," he said. "Don't look at me like that—it's true. Dad's a full Reaper, and he has no reason to spare *any* of the ghosts, including me."

"Only because he wouldn't stop long enough to listen." He was right, though. In my dad's eyes, I was betraying the very essence of being a Reaper by protecting the ghosts.

Mart gave a short laugh. "I guess it's not a huge deal if the Reapers get rid of some of the competition."

"You're a ghost, too, if you've forgotten."

"I'm tethered to you, not Hawkwood Hollow," he said. "If you ask me, the best thing to do is for the pair of us to go and lie low somewhere until the Reapers are gone."

"What about our employees?" Hell, our entire business depended upon the town's reputation as a haunted haven. "You don't want to be the only ghost left in town, do you? When we lived in ghost-free towns before, you did nothing but complain about how bored you were."

"Do you really think you can stop the whole council from coming here?" I heard the tremor in his voice. "If you stay, you know what they'll do to me."

I know. Dammit. "I'll try to reason with Dad. Let's hope old Harold is willing to lend a hand."

I assumed Harold would be back home by now, and I'd guessed right. The instant my fist hit the wooden door, he appeared with his scythe in hand. "Back already?"

"What are you doing with that?" I took a step back, eyeing the sharp instrument. "Not hunting the ghosts?"

"Of course not," he said. "If that vampire comes near the graveyard, I want to be prepared."

"You know he escaped then."

"Obviously," he growled. "Did you succeed in driving that Reaper father of yours in the opposite direction?"

"Ah… not exactly." My heart dipped a little. I'd really screwed up, and while it might take him some time to find the vampire, my dad was not the type to leave unfinished business behind him. Once he'd taken care of the vampire, he'd come back for Hawkwood Hollow.

Could one Reaper banish a town's worth of ghosts? Debatable, but if anyone was bound to give it a try, it was my dad.

"I knew it," said Harold. "I knew you'd bring the Reapers here."

"If not me, someone else would have," I said ineffectually. "Mina's put us on the map with her constant antics. She sent the vampire to draw the Reaper Council's attention, and I assume she ensured they picked my dad just to add insult to injury."

"Don't act like you haven't endangered us," he said. "There's a reason I worked so hard to ensure I was listed as the only Reaper contact in the town."

"Then why'd Shelton go to my dad and give away my location?" That part I still didn't understand. "If he hadn't— well, Dad would have come hunting for the vampire anyway, but he wouldn't have known my address."

Old Harold worked his jaw. "Shelton didn't say."

"Can't you call him and ask for clarification?" I folded my arms across my chest. "He doesn't want the council to come here, does he? He ought to be able to help convince my dad that the town's in good hands."

"I can't control what Shelton does," he growled. "I think he's being watched, in fact."

"By Mina?" Dread gripped my chest. "Is *he* the one she's been threatening?"

Was that why he'd gone to my dad? It still didn't explain why Dad had asked me to come home, but maybe I'd been unfair to assume an ulterior motive. He might have had a genuine change of heart.

Now, though? I'd risked more than my own future by drawing his attention to Hawkwood Hollow.

"I think the real question is, what are you going to do now?" asked Harold. "If you care for this town as much as you claim, you'll do your best to protect it."

"If you think I can argue with the entire Reaper Council, you're dead wrong. I couldn't even convince my dad to leave the town alone, and we're related."

"Then try harder." Beneath his irritation, I detected a hint of… Was that fear? "One sole Reaper I can handle but not the council."

"You handled Shelton. Why would my dad be any different?"

"That was supposed to be the end of it," he growled. "If you don't stop your father from making a mistake, it'll spell disaster for all of us."

I blinked. "I didn't think you cared for the ghosts that much."

"Fool." He backed into the doorway, gripping his scythe tightly. "It's not about the ghosts. It's about the stability of the entire afterworld."

What's he talking about?

"You've lost your mind," Mart informed him.

Dad's words came back to me. "He did say that a large number of deaths at one time could be destabilising—is that what this is about?"

In response, Harold swore at me and then slammed the door in our faces.

"That was weird." I turned to Mart. "What's with him? Did someone shove a scythe up his backside?"

"No, he's scared." Mart drifted backwards, away from the Reaper's cottage. "And I am too. I don't want to be banished."

"You won't be. We'll talk Dad out of bringing anyone else here."

"Like you talked him out of poking his nose into our business?"

"All right, I screwed up." I threw up my hands. "But this was always going to happen when he found out where I lived, and I wanted to break the news on my own terms. We'll catch the vampire first, and then—"

"Go ahead." Mart's eyes widened as he looked at a spot just past my shoulder. "He's right there."

"What?" I spun on my heel in time to catch the blurred figure of the vampire vanishing from sight. "Hey!"

I broke into a run, then Mart overtook me.

"I'll catch him," he called over his shoulder.

I quickened my pace, confusion rising within me. Was the vampire trying to lure me into a trap? He had some serious nerve coming back into Hawkwood Hollow while everyone was on the lookout for him, but he was so damned *fast*. I'd already lost sight of him, though I ran as quickly as humanly possible.

Skidding into the high street, I saw a commotion outside the police station again. The crowd forced me to slow my pace and push my way through to the doors—where a figure lay inert on the floor in the lobby.

Drew.

14

"Drew!" I shouted his name, but he didn't move. My heart swooped down and then stuttered when he stirred, groaning. Had the vampire bitten him? There was a *lot* of blood.

I elbowed my way through the crowd, my nerves buzzing with fury. *The vampire attacked Drew.* Nothing else mattered. "Drew, are you okay? Drew?"

He didn't answer. Two paramedics had shown up and pushed their way to the front of the crowd, and I was too numb with shock to protest when they blocked me from reaching Drew.

When they moved him from the police-station lobby and down the road to the hospital, I tailed them, my mind whirling with questions. Why had the vampire attacked Drew? To hurt me, no doubt, but he'd taken a serious risk in coming back so soon after his last attack on the police station. No doubt the vampire had taken advantage of half the team being either in the hospital or outside the town searching for him.

That was the rational part of my brain talking. The irrational part wanted to seize that vampire and wring his neck. If I'd been able to track him through the afterworld, I might have done just that.

Instead, I forced myself to return to the police station in search of another officer to waylay for an explanation.

"Hey—you," I called to the shellshocked shifter receptionist. "Did you see what the vampire came back for? Did he have a guilty conscience and want to turn himself in?"

The receptionist shook her head, but someone else spoke from behind me.

"No, he came back for the book," said Wendy.

I whipped around. Wendy and Jennifer Ness had walked up behind me, the latter wearing an expression that reminded me, oddly, of a furious Reaper.

"Didn't he already have the book?" I glanced over at the hospital doors, torn between my desire to be at Drew's side and my equally potent determination not to let that vampire scumbag hurt him again.

"No," said Wendy. "He wanted you to think he did, but I— I was the one who stole it."

A moment of tense silence passed during which I stared at Wendy, certain I hadn't heard her right.

"*You?*" I finally said. "It was you all along?"

"Explain." Jennifer snapped out the word. "Now."

Wendy took a couple of steps back, not making eye contact with either of us. "I… I'd rather not discuss this here," she mumbled. "Not in public."

"In my office, then." Jennifer retreated, but I remained on the spot, still torn. *Drew.* But there was nothing I could do for him now. Wendy, though… If she was the one who'd taken the book, she'd better have a bloody good explanation.

I'm sorry, Drew. With a curse, I followed the two witches back towards their headquarters. I'd lost sight of Mart at some point, but he'd probably freaked out at all the blood and ran off.

Jennifer didn't say a word until we'd reached her office and closed the door, at which point she levelled Wendy with a glare. "Talk."

"I was the one who removed the book from Mina's office." Wendy spoke with her head down. "I… knew Mina was going to come for it eventually, and I knew she'd have a spare key for her office, so I took the book out of the cabinet first."

"And how exactly did you know Mina was going to come for the book at this precise moment?" Jennifer enquired.

"Priscilla." Wendy wrung her hands. "She told me—told me the vampire was in the area on Mina's orders to steal the book. She knew Mina had the illegal book in her possession, but she didn't know where it was hidden."

"And yet you didn't tell me." Jennifer took in a measured breath. "I would dearly like to know why."

"I knew you'd probably move the book into your own office," Wendy said. "And you'd be the first person the vampire would suspect. He'd never guess that I had it."

"Neither did I," I interjected, "which would have been nice to know, given that the police have been hunting for days, thinking the vampire hid it in the tunnels. And the vampire played along."

"I—I'm sorry." More hand-wringing ensued. "I didn't dare give away the truth. Vampires can read minds, you see."

"Not mine." I'd rather stupidly forgotten about that particular vampiric advantage, but both Reapers and ghosts were immune to mind-reading, so he wouldn't have been able to retrieve any information from our thoughts. "I wouldn't have given away a thing."

"I didn't know." Wendy flinched when her boss glowered

at her again. "I thought he'd be better off staying in jail regardless."

"But you knew he'd get out eventually, didn't you?" I asked. "And his first stop would be here."

Except it hadn't been. His first stop had been the police station. He'd attacked Drew to hurt me. Wasn't the book supposed to be his priority? Or had he been trying to help Mina's other allies escape jail? It seemed an odd choice, because he ought to know that the longer he stuck around, the higher were the odds that the Reapers would send someone to catch him.

Wendy's mouth turned down at the corners. "Priscilla—she told me that he wasn't just here for the book. She mentioned… something about Hawkwood Hollow being the key location for whatever Mina is planning."

"By 'whatever she's planning,' you don't just mean retaking leadership of the coven, do you?" I asked. "You mean with the book. Necromancy. Did you read any of it?"

"Of course not." She flinched. "It's dark magic… horrible stuff. Enough to give you nightmares."

"*I* read some of the book," Jennifer said. "However, there's nothing to explain exactly what Mina planned to do with the information. I gather that most of the strongest necromancy is of great risk to the person who uses it."

"That was why she had her underlings summon demons and didn't do it herself." I spoke quickly, dread gripping my body as if I stood on the edge of a precipice over a sheer drop. "That's why it's restricted to Reapers. It's also why that book should have been handed over to the council at the first opportunity, but *you* decided not to tell the town's Reaper until it was already too late."

"It's not too late," Wendy whispered. "That's the point I'm making. I *have* the book. It's nowhere near Mina's hands. She hasn't won."

"Except there's a vampire on the loose attacking people at will," I pointed out. "I don't think *we've* won either. Where'd you even put the book?"

Wendy hesitated then pulled out her wand. "I… hid it at home, but I can bring it back here."

"Don't," Jennifer ordered. "No, if it hasn't been discovered yet, it's better to leave it where it is. The vampire is likely to come here to look for it sooner rather than later."

"Where *is* he?" Why not come into the coven's headquarters while he'd already been in the centre of town? Had he guessed that someone else had taken the book? "There aren't that many other obvious hiding places. Did he think the police had the book?"

"He might have," Wendy said. "Ah—if he couldn't read your thoughts, he'd have had no idea where the book was and would have had to guess. The only other people he spoke with were the police officers, right?"

"And Mina's allies in jail, I assume." Disconcerted, I turned back to the coven leader. "You read some of the book, did you?"

"Yes, and little of it surprised me," she said. "The majority of necromancy involves summoning from the afterworld, but I expect you're well aware of that already."

"Obviously." Except my own knowledge was limited by where I'd left off in my apprenticeship. "She's already tried summoning demons, but that doesn't require her to be in a particular location."

Wendy gave a violent shudder. "Priscilla… She hinted that Hawkwood Hollow is particularly—I mean, places that have seen a lot of death are often used for rituals."

"I gathered," Jennifer said quietly. "But surely even Mina wouldn't be *that* foolish."

"You'd be surprised." I thought of the tunnels, of the Reaper's warning, and of my dad's words—*Mina Devlin might have destabilised the entire afterworld.* "How much do you know about the floods twenty years ago?"

My words hung in the air like a spirit conjured from beyond the grave, while Jennifer frowned at me. I didn't know her precise age, but at the time of the floods, she'd have been a teenager. Certainly old enough to remember.

"What are you implying?" she asked. "Is this to do with those tunnels?"

"Yes—probably," I said. "I don't know all the details of what Mina was doing in there, but I find it suspicious that the tunnels are located directly underneath the river that flooded and killed over a hundred people over two decades ago, yet nobody has ever discovered them until now."

"You weren't here," Wendy said tremulously. "Nobody went near the river for weeks after the floods."

"Really?" I surveyed the coven leader. "Wouldn't the authorities have wanted to search for survivors? Where was Mina?"

"From what I remember, she led the evacuation of the coven," Jennifer said slowly, as if she was thinking hard. "Really, I have my doubts that Mina was responsible for a natural disaster."

"She was." The words tangled in my throat. I'd told nobody my suspicions. I hadn't even told Drew. Maybe if I had, he wouldn't be fighting for his life right now. "Old Harold told me. He lost his apprentice in the floods, so he'd know."

Jennifer and Wendy both gaped at me.

"The Reaper told you that?" Jennifer spoke first. "He lost his apprentice… Yes, I'd forgotten that, and I expect that was traumatising for him, but…"

"It's true," I pressed. "Mina was trying to—honestly, I'm not sure *what* she and the coven were doing. He didn't give me the details. But we already know Mina used the floods to cover up murders, and most powerful forms of necromancy require sacrifices."

Wendy let out a whimper and backed away towards the door. Jennifer, for her part, studied me for a moment and then took a measured breath. "I'll ask the Reaper for clarification, but that'll have to wait until later. We need to find this vampire."

Right. Focus on the present. I wrenched my thoughts back to our current dilemma. "The vampire—if he was a wizard when he was alive, he might even have been directly involved with the coven's actions twenty years ago. He'll certainly know what Mina's planning."

"Nevertheless," Jennifer said, "we have to be prepared for him to come here searching for the book. Wendy, you should go home and lie low. I'll deal with the vampire."

"How exactly do you plan to do that?" I couldn't even track him with my Reaper skills. How was a witch supposed to find him?

At that moment, a loud scream rang out from somewhere below our feet. The three of us all moved towards the door at the same time, and I took the lead as we ran downstairs and out into the lobby.

There, Priscilla lay in a bloody heap in front of the door to Mina's office, unmoving.

"The vampire!" I looked around wildly, but of course he'd disappeared. Jennifer stood rigid behind me, while Wendy swayed on the spot and then fell into a dead faint.

That's not good.

A creaking noise drew my attention to Mina's office, and the door swung open. Jennifer saw, too, and we both ran towards the door.

When we burst into the room, the vampire bared his teeth in a grin. He was seated behind Mina's old desk. "I believe I have the upper hand. I don't suppose you'd like to hand over the book?"

"We don't have it." I didn't dare take my eyes off the vampire to look at Jennifer, but my hand crept towards my pocket for my wand.

Jennifer whipped out her own wand and cast a spell that knocked Mina's desk askew but failed to make contact with its target. The vampire moved fast, darting out and into the lobby like smoke, and he appeared at the foot of the stairs with a smirk on his face. "Is it upstairs, I wonder?"

"You're welcome to look." Jennifer took aim, but once again, her spell missed as the vampire sprang out of sight. "You're wasting your time here."

"Oh, I don't think so." The vampire flashed me a fanged smile. "I'm surprised the Reaper didn't go back to check on her other friends right away, rather than leaving them vulnerable to an attack."

"What?" *Jia. Allie.* "What did you do?"

His smile widened. "Bring the book to the tunnel within one hour, or they die. That's my condition, Reaper."

15

I lunged at the vampire, but he vanished at a speed that rivalled my own ability to move through shadows. With a curse, I jumped into the afterworld, aiming for the bridge.

I'd overlooked his desire to hurt my allies, and now he had my friends held captive. This was all my fault. *Who did he take? Jia? Allie? Please, not Carey.*

I emerged from darkness and landed on the bridge. As I did so, my dad landed on the bridge in front of me, a menacing figure holding a scythe. "Maura. This place is swimming in death."

"I'm aware." Crap. He couldn't have shown up at a worse time. "Can you wait there a moment? And please don't Reap any souls while I'm gone."

"What are you talking about?" He lifted his scythe, eyeing a couple of terrified-looking ghosts near the bank. "I wouldn't be much of a Reaper if I ignored this flagrant dereliction of duty."

"Not the time!" I held out my arm in a futile attempt to block his path. "The vampire has taken my friends hostage in exchange for a certain book, and if I don't get into that tunnel—"

"This town is in a terrible state, Maura."

"Then I'm the one you want to talk to," growled a voice.

I never thought I'd be relieved to see Harold the Reaper. He'd appeared at the bridge's other side, his own scythe held aloft. Harold caught my eye briefly, which I judged to mean he had the situation handled, then returned his attention to my dad.

I, meanwhile, sprinted towards the inn. A commotion had broken out inside the restaurant, and I snagged the arm of a passing wizard to ask what had happened.

"This guy ran in, grabbed the girl working at the counter, and left!" he said. "He grabbed the woman, too—you know, the one who owns the place."

Jia and Allie. "Did he grab a girl as well? A teenager?"

"I… didn't see." He backed away as I stalked past into the lobby. My brother zipped over, his expression unusually downcast.

"I reckon Carey's hiding," he told me. "She wasn't downstairs when you left earlier, and Allie wouldn't have let the vampire take her."

"There wasn't much she could have done to stop him." Damn. I sure *hoped* Harold would be able to keep my dad from massacring the local ghosts, because I had no choice but to turn my back on the two Reapers if I wanted to help my friends.

But to do so… I needed that book.

"You aren't seriously thinking of giving that guy what he wants?" Mart asked.

"You know I don't have a choice." Even if the vampire was bluffing, it wasn't a risk I could afford to take. "Can you do me a favour and go warn the other ghosts to hide? If Harold can't stop Dad from getting at them, I don't want them paying the price for my mistake."

Mart scowled. "Fine."

He vanished into the games room, while I took a deep breath and leapt through the shadows, this time landing in the witches' headquarters again.

Wendy exclaimed at the sight of me and shrank back when I stalked towards her.

"The vampire wants the real book in exchange for sparing Jia and Allie," I said. "He has them held hostage in the tunnels."

"I—can't give it to you," Wendy said tremulously.

"It's the only way." I looked at Jennifer, who shook her head. "He's not willing to negotiate. I won't let him actually *take* the book."

"It's too risky." Jennifer glanced behind her at the door to Mina's office. "Besides, Wendy hid the book at home."

"Did you have an alternative?" A cursory scan of the lobby told me that someone had removed Priscilla and cleaned up the bloodstains she'd left on the floor, but Mina's office door remained ajar. "If Jia and Allie die because of your decision to withhold the truth from me, you won't get any support from me when Mina returns to take over the coven. That, I can promise you."

Wendy flinched. "I… I can get the book."

She pulled out her wand and gave it a wave, casting a transportation spell. As she disappeared in a swirl of light, Jennifer and I were left facing one another across the lobby.

"Did Priscilla survive?" I finally asked.

"Barely." Jennifer's lips compressed. "This is a terrible plan, Maura. It's not even a plan at all."

"Sorry for not coming up with something better when two of my friends are being held hostage, and there's a

Reaper waiting to skewer every single ghost in town with his scythe the instant I turn my back on him."

Her brows rose. "A Reaper?"

"The bloody council sent one of their Reapers to hunt the vampire." I decided not to mention he was a relation. "If we'd known the vampire didn't have the book, we could have delivered him to the council in person without any need for this."

Wendy reappeared in another flash, clutching a worn leather-bound volume to her chest. "I… Here it is."

"Thanks for that." I tried to grab the book from her, but she held fast, refusing to let go. "Oh, for God's sake. Do you want to come and fight the vampire yourself, is that it?"

"Wendy." Jennifer spoke in a firm but gentle tone. "Give Maura the book."

I tugged again and managed to get the book free from Wendy's limp arms. "The vampire is in the tunnels. He's likely to make an escape through the other exit, so if you want to do something to help, be ready to ambush him."

I didn't wait for a reply. Holding the book tight to my chest, I jumped into the shadows of the afterworld. Brightness pierced my vision, and I squinted, realising the dazzling light shone from the book itself. *What the hell is that—a glow-in-the-dark spell?*

No time to stop and investigate. I pictured the interior of the tunnel's main chamber, and a moment later, my feet touched down on damp stone. Holding the book with one hand, I reached for my wand with the other to light up the gloom.

My wand-light shone on the vampire, who stood over the unconscious forms of Jia and Allie. The vampire smiled at me, his teeth glowing in the wand's light. "I'm glad you saw sense."

"Let them go first." I held up the book so he could see the

cover, which was no longer glowing. Weird—but again, I had no time to give it a closer look. "That was our deal."

"They're free." He took a gliding step to the side, gesturing to Jia and Allie with one hand and extending the other to take the book.

"Nice try." I didn't budge. "I want them out of here first."

"That wasn't part of the deal." He stepped forward in a blur, and before I could blink, he'd seized the leather-bound volume from my hand. "Thank you for this."

No, you don't. The shadows answered my unvoiced command, and before I'd quite figured out my plan, I'd pulled both him *and* the book into the afterworld.

As darkness folded around us, the vampire stood rigid with shock. Wrenching the book out of his grip, I gave him a firm shove, picturing the first place that came into my head.

The vampire bared his teeth with a snarl of fury, but I'd pushed him out of the shadows and into the rushing current of the river.

Have fun in there. I turned my back and stepped through the afterworld, emerging back into the chamber where I'd left the others. The darkness receded as I crouched down beside Jia and Allie. "Are you okay?"

"Yes," Jia groaned. "Please tell me you didn't give him the book."

"I didn't." I held up the leather-bound tome in demonstration. It'd be tricky to get the two of them out of here through the afterworld while holding the book at the same time, but I didn't want to leave them in the tunnel a moment longer.

I tucked the book under my arm and extinguished my wand's light before taking Jia's hand in mine and grabbing Allie's with my other. Shadows coiled around the three of us, and I pictured the inn's lobby in my mind's eye.

When we emerged into the light, Allie stirred, while Jia

blinked in surprise. "Thanks, Maura—but where's the vampire?"

"I may have dropped him in the river." There was a notable weight missing from under my arm. *Crap.* "And… dropped the book in the afterworld. I'll be right back."

Shadows folded around me again, and I scanned the afterworld for the worn-leather cover of the book. You'd think its bright glow would make it easy to spot, but there was no sign of it in the surrounding darkness.

"Oh no." I pictured the tunnel again. Upon emerging into the chamber from which I'd rescued the others, I pulled out my wand and cast a light spell that revealed no sign of the book in the tunnel either.

The vampire couldn't have stolen it when I dropped him in the river, could he?

Heart sinking, I stepped back into the shadows and emerged on the bridge beside the two Reapers. Neither Harold nor my dad seemed to have moved an inch in the time it'd taken me to rescue Jia and Allie from the vampire.

"Maura," Dad said through gritted teeth, "do you make a habit of using your powers so casually?"

"Only in an emergency—and this is one. We have a problem." I took in a breath. "The book. I may have dropped it in the afterworld."

"You did *what?*" said old Harold.

"I was trying to rescue two people at the same time," I protested. "I also threw the vampire into the river. Did either of you two see him?"

"No," Harold said. "We didn't."

Oh boy. I must have dropped him farther upstream, which should ideally mean the police would see him—or failing that, the witches, if they'd listened to my request to stop him from fleeing. But where was that book?

"Also," I said, "is it normal for books to glow when you take them into the afterworld?"

"Definitely not," Dad said darkly. "I gather that was why this one was so dangerous… and why it should never have been hidden from the council."

"Not my mistake." Shadows swept around my feet, smothering the bridge in the darkness of the afterworld. "Help me find it. Please."

"If it's not here"—Harold moved forward, his scythe held aloft—"someone else must have picked it up."

"Who?" Not many people could access the afterworld. Only Reapers… and ghosts, but most of them couldn't pick things up. "Not Mina, surely."

"An afterworld beast, perhaps," Dad said. "This isn't good. If someone attempts a ritual from the book too close to the nexus point—"

"What do you think I've been trying to tell you?" Harold interjected.

"Hold on." I lifted a hand. "What in hell is a nexus point?"

"In the afterworld," Harold said almost unwillingly. "It's—"

"That knowledge is for full Reapers only," Dad said.

"You were the one who wanted me to come back and resume my training," I snapped. "Tell me the truth."

"A nexus point is a location in *this* realm that is linked directly to the deeper levels of the afterworld without the usual gates and protections in the way," Harold told me. "That, Maura, is the result of what occurred here twenty years ago."

"I don't follow." The deeper levels of the afterworld… If a door *there* was open on top of us, wouldn't there be demons flooding the area instead of ghosts? "Was that what Mina did?"

"Briefly." The Reaper drew in a breath. "She and her

coven tried to conduct a ritual that would put them in contact with a greater demon of the afterworld, and the lives sacrificed during the floods were intended to open a nexus point. Until I slammed the gates closed myself."

"It's an advanced Reaper skill," my dad said grudgingly. "Not one you reached in your training. Closing the doors of the afterworld so that no spirit can move on naturally—it's against our nature."

"I had no choice," said Harold. "If anyone tries to banish all the spirits currently in Hawkwood Hollow, it'll cause even more damage than the initial floods did. The whole town remains a nexus point, and the gates I closed with my own hand are the sole obstacle between any foolish practitioner and a catastrophe that would see the entire town opened to the deeper levels of the afterworld."

I took a step back, my mind reeling. "Did... Mina know you stopped her?"

"No," said Harold. "She always assumed the number of ghosts in town was a consequence of her failed ritual, not of me closing the doors to the afterworld myself. She never had much respect for Reapers."

"That will be her undoing," Dad said. "I'll find that vampire, and then I'll deal with this."

"And... the book?" My question went unanswered as he vanished from sight, leaving Harold and me alone. "Okay then."

I didn't expect *Harold* to exert himself to help, so I pictured the riverbank near the tunnel's other entrance and vanished through the afterworld. On the other side, I found several police officers cowering away from my dad. He was back in his terrifying Reaper form, wreathed in shadows and wielding his scythe.

"Dad—stop freaking people out." I ran towards him. "Is the vampire...?"

"He's not in the river… and neither is that book."

Not good. "Where'd he go?"

Vampires weren't trackable through the afterworld, and he'd have long since outrun the police officers. It didn't look as though any witches had come here like I'd asked, either, but I did have one ace—or rather, ghost—up my sleeve.

Without delay, I hopped back into the shadows and pictured the inn's lobby. Mart's aggrieved-looking ghost greeted me on the other side. "Where are you going this time?"

"The vampire escaped." I breathed in and out, my heart racing. "Listen—I have an idea."

"This I'd like to hear."

"Oi." I looked for the others and saw Jia and Allie sitting at the foot of the stairs, both of them looking shaken but relieved to be out of the tunnel. "Did you tell the ghosts to hide?"

"Obviously," Mart said. "They don't want dear old Dad to eviscerate them."

"Yeah, there's an issue," I said. "We need to find that vampire, and ghosts can move faster than humans."

"I've been trying to tell you that for years."

"What I mean to say is that I need their help," I said. "I can't track that vampire in the afterworld, and I can't be in several places at once. If you and the other ghosts help, though, there might be a chance of stopping the Reapers from sinking this place and all the ghosts along with it."

That would depend on whether Dad was in a generous mood, but Harold's revelation might have convinced him to put his plan to turn us in to the Reaper Council on hold.

"I can't stop that vampire either." He stuck his transparent hand through my forehead, causing a full-body shiver to run down my spine. "This is what'll happen if I try to grab him."

"You can slow him down, can't you?" I pressed. "I can't

imagine he'd find it very fun to have a bottle of water dumped on his head, any more than I did. Use your imagination. Make yourself indispensable, and the Reapers will have to let you stay. Do you understand?"

A grin split his face. "Oh yes. I'll give him hell."

As he vanished, I spied Harold approaching the inn's automatic doors and went out to meet him. "Got an idea?"

"Have you ever Reaped a vampire's soul before?"

"No." I knew it could be done, but I usually forgot they even *had* souls.

"I expect you quit before you reached that stage of your training," he went on. "You might want to borrow this."

He held out his scythe. I stared for a moment, then I took it, mostly because I didn't know what else to do. "Thanks. I think."

Dad had a head start on me, but he didn't have the help of a few dozen ghosts. I spied more spirits gathering on the riverbank, perhaps drawn there by the commotion.

"Hey." I ran to them, and the ghosts recoiled from the scythe in my hands. "Wait—I'm not going to Reap your souls. I need your help. There's a vampire on the loose, and if we don't catch him, the other Reaper will come back."

"I saw him," one of the ghosts said hesitantly. "Heading north around the outskirts of the town."

North, really? Was the vampire planning on coming back into town through the northern route, or was he just trying to confuse everyone? "Thanks. I'll find him."

"Not without me." Mart appeared at my back. "I've asked the ghosts to spread the word as far as possible… Wow, you have a scythe."

"I do." I readied myself. "You really want to come?"

"Obviously." He eyed the scythe warily. "I'll catch you up. I don't want you to accidentally decapitate me."

"I'm going north." I stepped into shadow, picturing the road leading around the eastern edge of town.

When I emerged, I didn't see the vampire, but Mart was already waiting with a smug smile on his face. Ghosts really could move fast, and they weren't restricted by having to constantly jump in and out of the afterworld like I was.

"I thought you'd take all day." He zoomed ahead of me while I took another step through shadow. It helped that the scythe didn't weigh anything, but the deserted country lanes were devoid of other ghosts to ask for help.

The next time I emerged, Mart waited on the other side, and he pointed north. "He went up there. I tried to get in his way, but he laughed at me."

"Scumbag." I hopped into shadow and out, once again finding no vampire on the other side.

Mart was there, wearing a scowl on his face. "He's toying with us. He keeps changing directions."

"Looking for the book?"

"About that—" He cut off with a yelp. "Incoming!"

My head snapped upward as a gust of wind blew overhead. A broomstick appeared in the sky, heading south, and atop it sat a witch with long flowing dark hair and a billowing grey cloak.

Mina Devlin.

My jaw dropped. I hadn't expected to see her here, out in the open. Hadn't believed she'd leave herself vulnerable in that way. After all, my scythe worked on all humans, and while it was questionable as to whether she had a conscience, she certainly had a soul.

A smile inexplicably came to my mouth. *Get down here, and we'll see which of us comes out on top.*

"You!" She pointed her wand at me without descending from the sky. "You won't get away this time."

As she cast her spell, I flung myself into shadow and reappeared below her broomstick. She was high enough off the ground to prevent me from reaching her with my scythe—in theory. There was no law preventing me from Reaping someone's soul up in the air, as long as I timed it right.

I pictured Mina's face and stepped into the shadows, appearing above her broomstick. As I began to fall, I angled myself so that my scythe would strike her on the way down.

A solid force knocked me out of the air. I fell—too fast— and while the shadows broke my fall, I slammed onto my back. The breath fled my lungs, leaving me gasping for air with stars winking before my eyes. Through blurred vision, I saw Mina's broomstick circle overhead and her wand move as she took aim again—but her spell fizzled out.

A second broomstick had appeared from the direction of Hawkwood Hollow, and its rider was Jennifer Ness. She flew towards us, her wand in her hand and a determined expression on her face.

Was that her plan? A midair duel with wands was risky for both participants, especially if Mina had made herself immune to regular spells as well as to Reapers. She'd bought me time, though, so I pushed upright and picked up the scythe.

"Maura!" shouted my brother.

I spun around, seeing him chasing a fleeing figure. *That vampire.* I flung myself through the shadows and emerged next to Mart, joining his pursuit of the vampire. At least a dozen ghosts floated alongside my brother, flinging stones and other projectiles at their target.

"You!" I jabbed a finger at the vampire. "What's wrong? Scared of a few ghosts?"

"He's absolutely terrified." Mart snickered. "Get him, Maura."

I picked up the pace, swinging the scythe as I did so. The vampire avoided my strike, and a flurry of bright lights from the sky above distorted my vision. The witches' duel raged on, and I didn't dare look up to see who was winning.

Another swing of the scythe had the vampire on the retreat. The ghosts followed him, and the vampire let out a cry of rage when one of the sizeable rocks they threw hit him square in the forehead. His slowed pace enabled me to catch up, raising the scythe again. Yet the ghosts didn't move away. Did they trust me to hit the vampire and not them? Even Mart waited expectantly, and the show of trust in me brought unexpected warmth to my chest.

With another swing, the scythe hit the vampire head-on, causing him to stagger and then fall into a heap. I couldn't tell if I'd cut out his soul or not, but above my head, Mina shrieked, "You'll pay for that! Everyone you love will die!"

I lifted my head to see Mina clearly winning the fight; Jennifer's broomstick had lost altitude but hadn't fallen out of the air yet. "Come and get me, then."

"Stop."

The chilling voice signalled the arrival of another Reaper, casting all of us in darkness that spread upward until it almost reached the two broomsticks in flight. If I hadn't known it was my dad, I'd have been equally cowed at the sight of the afterworld itself cloaking the Reaper's menacing figure.

"Stop," Dad repeated. "This town is under my protection."

Whoa.

The darkness receded a little, revealing the crumpled form of the vampire. Dad stepped up, lifted his scythe, and brought it down with precision.

The vampire... fell apart. That was the only way I could describe the sight of his body dissolving on the spot as if it were nothing more than an illusion. His unoccupied clothes fell into a heap as he turned to ashes, and I could have sworn

I saw something ghostlike emerge and drift away into the afterworld, fading from sight.

"Dammit!" Mart said from behind me. "She's gone."

I lifted my head as the darkness ebbed a little more, revealing a sky that was notably empty of broomsticks. I spied Jennifer a short distance away where she'd landed on the hillside, but Mina had disappeared.

"She knew she was outnumbered," I guessed. "I hope it wasn't one of her allies who took that book."

"You still haven't found the book?" Dad sounded more like himself again, having lowered his scythe and pulled back a bit on the scary Grim Reaper vibes.

"Actually…" With a flourish, Mart produced the book from behind him and dropped it at Dad's feet. "You're welcome."

16

I'd never seen Dad as speechless as I did when Mart threw the missing book down before him. He was still for a moment, while Mart smirked. "What? Don't tell me you thought a ghost couldn't pick up a book. You should know better."

Recovering, my dad bent to retrieve the leather-bound book and then glanced over at Jennifer, who was approaching us with her broomstick held in one hand. "Was that your former coven leader? I can see why you drove her out."

"Glad we're finally on the same page," I said. To Jennifer, I added, "Did you really expect to beat Mina in an outright duel?"

"I hoped she'd let down her guard," she replied. "Or give away her weaknesses."

"What's she done to make herself Reaper-proof, do you know?" The scythe had bounced clean off her.

"That shouldn't be possible," Dad told me.

"Clearly it is. The scythe had no effect on her." I studied

the book in his hand, recalling its glow in the afterworld. "Are you going to give that to the Reaper Council?"

"That's the intention."

I tensed. "Then… are you going to tell them about Hawkwood Hollow?"

"It's my responsibility."

"Did you not hear what old Harold said?" My grip on the scythe he'd given me tightened. "I'm inclined to believe he's telling the truth about this place being on top of a massive potential disaster, and the ghosts aren't doing any harm."

"Potential disaster?" Jennifer echoed. "Is this to do with what you mentioned—your theory about the cause of the floods?"

"It's no theory. It's fact," I replied. "Old Harold was there, so he should know."

"He's right," Dad said slowly, "but I'd also be risking disaster if I were to ignore such a major risk."

"I'm not ignoring the risk, but it's even riskier to try a major banishment on top of—what did you call it, a nexus point?"

His jaw twitched. "I didn't plan to try a mass banishment, but it's possible to deal with the situation using a more subtle approach."

"Subtle?" I echoed. "Meaning banishing the ghosts one at a time? Can you guarantee it won't inadvertently cause more trouble? As long as Mina Devlin is at large, we're potentially playing into her hands by meddling with the afterworld near Hawkwood Hollow."

"Yes…" A pause. "I'll talk to the council and report this witch as a danger to all of us."

"If you mention the town's name, you know what they'll do."

"They won't come in person," he said. "They'll send an ambassador, like Shelton."

"At least ask Harold first, before you risk all our lives," I said. "He and Shelton both understand the situation, but please, for everyone's sakes, don't bring the council into this."

"What if the council could help you find your runaway witch?" he enquired.

"No." I shook my head. "I don't need to find her. She'll find me."

Of that I had no doubt.

"She's right," Jennifer said, having maintained a baffled silence throughout this part of our conversation. "Mina has a personal grudge against Maura that will no doubt have worsened now that her vampire ally is dead."

"She does." I swivelled to my dad. "Look, my boyfriend was attacked and left for dead, and the vampire also kidnapped two of my friends and left them traumatised. Can I *please* go and see if they're all right before you walk into town and start banishing our ghosts?"

"They aren't *your* ghosts, Maura."

"Have you forgotten how they helped you chase down that vampire?" I gestured to Mart. "The ghosts in Hawkwood Hollow have been around for years. They deserve to have a say in their own fates, you know."

"Maura." He sighed. "Ghosts don't have rights. I'd have thought you'd remember at least some of your training."

"Hey!" Mart objected. "I don't have rights, do I? I'm as much a person as you are."

"Ghosts are echoes of a person, nothing more," Dad said, without looking at my brother.

"He saved my life," I told him. "Mart did. When the witches had me trapped down in that tunnel and turned off my Reaper skills, leaving me for dead, my bond with Mart let me contact him so he could let me out."

"Nevertheless." He sighed again. "I'm not heartless enough to sever your connection, but I can't allow the town to remain a hub for spirits who have lingered far beyond their time."

"Then wait until later." I cursed the pleading note in my voice. "Speak to Harold and Shelton first. Find Mina. Forget the ghosts, for the time being, until she's dealt with."

He inclined his head. "Very well."

I hadn't won… but I hadn't lost yet either.

———

Several minutes later, I entered the hospital ward and zeroed in on Drew's voice. From his tone, he appeared to be arguing with the hospital staff about being confined to bed.

"I'm fine," he was saying to an unimpressed nurse. "This is unnecessary. There are others in worse shape than I am."

"Drew!" I ran across the room and hugged him awkwardly across the hospital bed, ignoring the nurse's look of disapproval. "Are you okay?"

"No," said the nurse, whom I belated recognised as Cathy. "He keeps trying to get out of bed and reopen his wounds."

"That's because I have a duty to keep my officers informed of—wait." He squinted at me. "Maura, where's the vampire?"

"The vampire's dead," I said. "Deader than undead, I mean. The Reaper took his soul."

He raised a brow. "I didn't know that was possible."

"It's just trickier than for the average person," I replied. "Also, Mina Devlin showed up. Can we talk alone?"

I was abruptly conscious of the other people in the room—including Petra, who was either unconscious or asleep. Still, that didn't mean I trusted her not to eavesdrop on me, given half a chance.

"No," Cathy said flatly. "You're not taking any of my patients away, Reaper."

"I didn't say I was, and I also just saved the town from potential disaster."

"And guess who's going to have to clean up the mess?" She grunted and turned away. "Don't you even think about leaving, Detective."

"Wouldn't dream of it," Drew muttered. "Isn't she the coven healer?"

"Yep." I moved closer to the bed and took his hand. "I'm glad you're all right. I didn't want to leave you here. I'm sorry."

"Taking out the vampire was more important."

"That was my dad, not me," I said. "And Mart was the one who swiped the book before Mina could steal it back."

My brother had gone back to the inn. He didn't like hospitals any more than he liked morgues or graveyards.

"Good." He shifted position on the pillows, and I glimpsed the distinct bite marks on his arms and neck. "This is embarrassing. I thought I could take a vampire."

"He was relying on the element of surprise." A lump grew in my throat. "And—he targeted you to get at me. He captured Jia and Allie too. I should have known he wouldn't just go for the book without getting in a few hits first."

"Don't blame yourself for this—it's my job to apprehend criminals." He tightened his grip on my hand. "Also, I'm hearing rumours. Did Jennifer and Mina really duel on broomsticks?"

"That rumour spread fast," I remarked. "They did, but it ended at a stalemate. Mina got away."

"And your father?"

"I managed to convince him to prioritise catching Mina over our ghostly situation." I spoke in a low voice. "For now. I'm hoping Shelton and Harold will work their powers of persuasion on him and convince him to find another solution."

"I imagine that would depend on whether Mina tries anything else that draws the Reapers' attention."

"Yeah." That was what I was afraid of, but I kept my misgivings to myself then looked closer at Drew. Despite his determination to sit upright, his exhaustion was obvious. "It's over for now. You should rest."

"I will," he said. "Once I've told the other officers the vampire is dead."

"Someone else can tell them that," I insisted. "If anyone comes in here to pester you, tell them to direct all questions to old Harold. He deserves being hassled more than you do, even if he did loan me his scythe."

"He did?"

"Yeah, I know." I moved closer and hugged him again. "Seriously. I thought you were dead when I saw you."

"Sorry." He hugged me back, wincing a little. "I'll definitely think twice before taking on a vampire in my human form again."

"With luck, he was Mina's only undead ally." I reluctantly let him go. "I have to go back to the inn and tell the others I'm okay, but I'll be back."

"I won't be in here much longer," he said. "They want to keep me overnight, but that's out of the question."

"Oh, is it?" I frowned at him. "Listen to the hospital staff. You're not invincible."

He grinned. "Speak for yourself."

"What's so funny?"

"I'm usually the one who's panicking over your half-dead body," he said. "It's a refreshing change."

"Oi." I swatted him on his uninjured arm, careful not to hit too hard. "If you stay put overnight, I'll ask my dad to include you in his meeting with the Reapers tomorrow."

"That's... not the most persuasive argument, Maura," he

said. "You're supposed to promise me a date, not a meeting with angels of death."

"We can do that too." I took in a breath. "There's something important I have to tell you, but I'd rather not do it publicly. We can discuss everything with the Reapers."

"That sounds ominous."

"It is." No point in underplaying the issue. "I have your curiosity now, right? Now stay put, or else I'll jump through the afterworld and return you to your hospital bed myself."

"Understood." His smile was back, though tinged with weariness. "I'll see you later. And… please don't get into any more fights while I can't help you."

"I won't." And for once, I meant it.

———

Back at the inn, I found that Jia and Allie had mostly recovered from their ordeal at the vampire's hands, while Carey had emerged unscathed from where she'd been hiding in her room.

I was intensely relieved that the vampire had spared her from his attempt to blackmail me, though it turned out the ghosts had been guarding her room diligently even before Mart had told them to help me out.

By the time I'd finished telling them all everything, my voice was raw, and I hadn't even reached the part about the floods yet. In truth, I wanted to wait until after I'd told Drew and discussed it with the Reapers before deciding how much to tell the others about the reasons for the town's overabundance of ghosts.

"Is someone going to banish us?" Vicky asked tremulously. She and the other ghosts had gathered around the table in the restaurant where I sat with Jia and the others, equally entranced by my story.

"No." For Allie and Carey's benefit, I added, "Ah—the Reapers aren't going to banish any of the ghosts. They've decided to prioritise hunting down Mina Devlin."

"Glad they've seen sense," Jia said. "And there are no more vampires hiding in the tunnels?"

"As far as I know," I said. "They're loners, so it's unlikely that Mina would have recruited more than one."

She'd have other allies, but Priscilla was still in critical condition at the hospital and unable to give us more information about the events that had put her on the vampire's tail. For now, we'd have to assume Jacob Reed had been the sole undead interloper in town.

"Good." Carey shuddered. "I'm glad you're all okay, but Drew... He's hurt, right?"

My chest tightened. "Yes, but he's going to be fine. If he stays put like I told him to and doesn't keep trying to leave the hospital ward, that is."

"What about the other officers?" Allie asked. "That Petra..."

"Oh, the vampire got her too." I had considerably more trouble feeling sorry for *her*. "She was responsible for his escape, so it serves her right."

"Yes, it does," said Jia. "Oh yeah—where'd Mina's evil book of necromancy end up?"

"With the Reaper Council," I said. "They'll keep it secure, so there won't be any more unexpected break-ins."

"And the coven leader will keep her word?" Allie queried. "She mentioned switching locations for the coven meetings."

"I'll have to ask her about that," I said. "I was going to persuade her to spare us from the coven's karaoke nights."

Jia snorted. "Yeah, I can live without those, thanks."

"Me too." I surveyed the others, my attention lingering on the ghosts. "We'll be fine. Dad will come to realise that the town wouldn't be the same without its ghosts, and he already understands that finding Mina is more important."

"Good," Mart said. "I wouldn't want to miss out on our Halloween special."

Right. We had just over a week until the big night—which also happened to be the one night of the year when the boundaries between the waking world and the afterworld were thinnest.

Could we bring down Mina before then? Debatable, but I was willing to give it a try.

Drew, luckily, kept to his word. He was discharged from the hospital the following morning, after I'd had a surprisingly restful night's sleep on the heels of a movie night consisting of everyone's favourites back-to-back. At least nobody complained, and as a bonus, I'd successfully distracted the ghosts from the looming threat of the Reaper Council for the time being.

I didn't believe Dad would *intentionally* bring the council here, but I still worried that the Reapers might ask unwanted questions when he handed over Mina's book. It was with some trepidation that I went to meet the Reapers at old Harold's cottage, walking hand in hand with Drew. This wasn't exactly how I'd planned to introduce my boyfriend to my dad, mostly because I hadn't wanted him to meet my parents in the first place, but it had to be done.

"So romantic," I commented as we walked through the cemetery gates. "We'll have a proper date later, promise."

"Of course." Drew squeezed my hand. "I behaved myself last night and didn't leave the hospital. What about you?"

"I fell asleep in the middle of a marathon of *My Little Pony* followed by *Star Wars.*"

"Whose idea was that?"

"The ghosts' idea." I dropped my voice when we reached Harold's cottage. "Better not mention that in front of my dad. He's still a little touchy about me befriending the dead."

I knocked on Harold's door. The old Reaper answered, beckoning me through into the cramped living room. The scythe had returned to its old position as a coatrack, while in the living room, the two other Reapers sat in chairs amid the piles of old junk.

"Hey." I nodded to Shelton. "It's been a while."

"So it has." Drew eyed the tall Reaper suspiciously and then tensed when my dad pushed his hood down to reveal his face. "You… look just like Maura."

"That's my dad," I said as we took the two remaining seats in the crowded room. "Dad, meet Drew. He's the head of the police here, so I figured he ought to listen in on this."

"He's not the head of the coven," Shelton objected.

"Good," Harold growled. "I don't trust the witches with anything, but we could use someone in authority as a witness. Someone with influence."

Drew shifted in his seat next to me. I figured he was thinking about certain officers who did their best *not* to listen to him, but I'd have thought Petra would reconsider defying orders after she'd nearly died the last time she'd taken matters into her own hands.

"I'm going to tell Jennifer everything," I told the Reapers. "She already knows most of it, so there won't be anything new."

"Does she now?" Harold said. "You shared secrets with the coven that weren't yours to tell?"

"They're not very secret anymore, are they?" I folded my arms across my chest. "She deserves to know what her predecessor did."

"Maura," Drew said, "what *did* Mina do? I take it this was

what you didn't want to talk about in public?"

"With good reason," Harold snapped. "This will have repercussions. If the council gets involved…"

"They won't," I said, with a meaningful look at my dad. "Look—Drew, Mina caused the floods twenty years ago. That was what she did."

His mouth fell open. "She murdered all those people?"

"Indirectly, yes." I swivelled to old Harold. "She was doing something illegal in the tunnels. Trying to get into the afterworld. Care to tell me what, exactly, ended with her opening a gate into the deeper afterworld?"

"Summoning," he growled. "She intended to summon a greater demon. A rank five, the highest there is."

My heart gave a stutter. *A greater demon.* "A—rank five? Can a human do that?"

"With enough sacrifices, it's certainly possible," my dad said.

My blood chilled. "That was why she opened the afterworld widely enough to form a nexus point."

"But you stopped her." Shelton addressed Harold; from his questioning tone, the other Reaper hadn't told him all the details yet either. "Didn't you?"

"Not exactly," Harold said quietly. "My apprentice was the one who figured out what she was doing. He'd noticed a number of souls hanging around the river who hadn't died of natural causes, and when he figured out they were sacrifices, he informed me at once. I think that was what pushed her into attempting the summoning early."

"She was doing other small-scale summonings before that?" I grimaced. "Practise runs?"

"More or less," Harold said. "I only had my apprentice's word to go on, and he was terrified at attracting the wrath of the coven leader. Unfortunately, by the time I reached the river, it was already too late."

"And then?" asked my dad. "You acted against Mina?"

"I did," he said. "I called upon all the skills I had in my possession to force the gates to the afterworld closed."

"That must have cost you," Shelton said quietly.

"It did," Harold said. "I was unconscious for days, and I woke up to find that the gates closing had had unintended side effects. Some of the victims of the floods had moved on —including my apprentice—but the rest were trapped in *this* world. I swiftly realised that it was a futile effort to banish them all one at a time. It wouldn't solve the underlying issue."

"So you retired instead of informing the council," Dad said accusingly.

"What would they have done?" he challenged. "They wouldn't have believed me. They never liked me, and thanks to Mina Devlin's propaganda, they wouldn't have known the coven was responsible. Unless they tried a mass banishment themselves, which would then have ripped the gates open again. No doubt they'd have blamed me or my apprentice instead of the coven."

Silence followed his outburst. I'd never heard him say so much at once, and he looked somewhat startled at his own audacity.

"A mass banishment isn't an option," said my dad. "However, there are… ways to fix the damage."

"With more than one Reaper," Shelton added. "You'd need a sizeable group to close such a rift in the afterworld."

"I wasn't willing to take the risk," said Harold. "If I picked the wrong person to entrust with the truth, it'd be a disaster. None of you saw what it was like. Half the population of the village drowned and their ghosts swarming the place—and the person responsible was in charge of the entire coven. I always wondered if she'd try again. I almost hoped she would so I'd no longer feel the burden of keeping her secret."

"You're a selfish individual," said my dad. "And Shelton—you kept his secret too?"

"I didn't know the extent of it," he said, "but I believed the town was in good hands with Harold and Maura."

I blinked in surprise, but Drew spoke up from next to me. "I agree. Mina is no longer in charge, so we don't have to worry about her using her power and influence over the town. And my networks have been working extensively to track her location over the last few months."

"Will she be able to try another summoning without the book?" I queried. "Was that what she planned to do—rip the gates open again and finish the job?"

"No doubt," growled Harold. "The book is now with the council, so she'll have to work from memory."

"Can't she get a copy from somewhere else?"

"There isn't one," he said. "I expect she got that one from the Founders—they're known for hoarding books that are supposed to belong to the Reapers."

"Who are the Founders?"

Dad made an impatient noise. "If I'm to keep your secret, I need to have a story for the council that won't end in my own punishment for your mistakes. Tell me everything about this coven leader… and about her allies."

"And don't leave me out of this either," I added. "I'd like to know how she repelled your scythe, Harold. That's not something a human should be able to do."

As he opened his mouth to speak, a scream rang out from somewhere in the distance, shrill and horrified.

"What… what was that?" I jumped to my feet and overtook Drew on the way to the door, though he was close on my heels when we emerged from the Reaper's cottage.

A second scream sounded when we reached the gates.

"What's going on over there?" I took off at a run, tracking the noise as having come from the coven's headquarters.

The doors slid open to let me inside as a third scream came echoing upstairs. Now I recognised its owner—Wendy.

I took the stairs two at a time and skidded to a halt at Jennifer's office. Inside, Wendy crouched on the floor, clutching a piece of paper in her hands.

"Wendy?" I asked. "What—?"

"She's gone," she whimpered. "She's gone."

"Jennifer?" My heart lurched. "When?"

"She didn't show up here this morning," she mumbled. "And I found this. Look."

I took the paper from her and read the words, *Thank you for the help, Maura. I'll trade your coven leader back if you give me the book. You have until Samhain night.*

"Not this again." I looked to Drew, whose expression was as grim as my own. "I guess Mina has played her hand."

And she'd taken the coven leader as a hostage for a reason… to send a message to the other witches. *You're next.*

"Why Samhain?" Drew asked.

My throat went dry. "Because it's the night when the veil between this world and the afterworld is thinnest."

If I were Mina, I'd pick that date to attempt the ritual. That was why she wanted the book.

After a short pause, Drew said, "We can't placate her. The book is gone."

"Good luck to her if she thinks she can pry it out of the Reaper Council's hands."

If we didn't trade the book for Jennifer, would Mina still be able to attempt the ritual? She might, and I didn't believe for an instant she intended to let Jennifer go. She wanted leadership of the coven back—and she wanted me gone too.

Too bad for her. I wasn't going anywhere, and I'd fight to my last breath to defend Hawkwood Hollow and the people there.

It's on, Mina.

ABOUT THE AUTHOR

Elle Adams lives in the middle of England, where she spends most of her time reading an ever-growing mountain of books, planning her next adventure, or writing. Elle's books are humorous mysteries with a paranormal twist, packed with magical mayhem.

She also writes urban and contemporary fantasy novels as Emma L. Adams.

Find out more about Elle's books at: https://www.elleadamsauthor.com/

Find Elle on Facebook at https://www.facebook.com/pg/ElleAdamsAuthor/